THE BARBARA CARTLAND ETERNAL COLLECTION

The Barbara Cartland Eternal Collection is the unique opportunity to collect all five hundred of the timeless beautiful romantic novels written by the world's most celebrated and enduring romantic author.

Named the Eternal Collection because Barbara's inspiring stories of pure love, just the same as love itself, the books will be published on the internet at the rate of four titles per month until all five hundred are available.

The Eternal Collection, classic pure romance available worldwide for all time .

I0626641

THE DAWN OF LOVE

Barbara Cartland

Barbara Cartland Ebooks Ltd

This edition © 2019

ISBNs

9781788671774   EPUB
9781788671781   PAPERBACK

Book design by M-Y Books
m-ybooks.co.uk

THE LATE DAME BARBARA CARTLAND

Barbara Cartland, who sadly died in May 2000 at the grand age of ninety eight, remains one of the world's most famous romantic novelists. With worldwide sales of over one billion, her outstanding 723 books have been translated into thirty six different languages, to be enjoyed by readers of romance globally.

Writing her first book 'Jigsaw' at the age of 21, Barbara became an immediate bestseller. Building upon this initial success, she wrote continuously throughout her life, producing bestsellers for an astonishing 76 years. In addition to Barbara Cartland's legion of fans in the UK and across Europe, her books have always been immensely popular in the USA. In 1976 she achieved the unprecedented feat of having books at numbers 1 & 2 in the prestigious B. Dalton Bookseller bestsellers list.

Although she is often referred to as the 'Queen of Romance', Barbara Cartland also wrote several historical biographies, six autobiographies and numerous theatrical plays as well as books on life, love, health and cookery. Becoming one of Britain's most popular media personalities and dressed in her trademark pink, Barbara spoke on radio and television about social and political issues, as well as making many public appearances.

In 1991 she became a Dame of the Order of the British Empire for her contribution to literature and her work for humanitarian and charitable causes.

Known for her glamour, style, and vitality Barbara Cartland became a legend in her own lifetime. Best remembered for her wonderful romantic novels and loved by millions of readers worldwide, her books remain treasured for their heroic heroes, plucky heroines and traditional values. But above all, it was Barbara Cartland's overriding belief in the positive power of love to help, heal and improve the quality of life for everyone that made her truly unique.

AUTHOR'S NOTE

George Bernard Shaw published his play, *Pygmalion*, in 1913.

This story of a flower girl trained by a phonetician to pass as a lady, although a most effective satire upon the English class system, is less a play of ideas than are Shaw's other major plays.

Its rich human content made it a favourite with the public both as a musical on the stage and on the screen with Rex Harrison and Audrey Hepburn in the leading parts.

Cecil Beaton's exquisite decor and dresses greatly contributed to its success and Eliza Doolittle is one of Shaw's unforgettable personalities.

CHAPTER ONE
1913

The Honourable Peregrine Gillingham jumped out of the hansom carriage, paid the cabby and walked up the steps of Windlemere House.

The front door was already open and he handed his tall hat to a footman who wore a powdered wig and then he nodded to the butler.

"Good evening, Dawkins."

"Good evening, sir."

"Is His Grace in the library?"

"Yes, sir, he's been waiting for nearly an hour."

There was a touch of rebuke in the butler's well-modulated voice and Peregrine smiled to himself as he followed the servant's rather pompous tread across the marble hall.

Windlemere House of all the magnificent mansions in Park Lane was the most outstanding.

It had been built by the Duke's grandfather and was the early Victorians' idea of what a Ducal house should look like.

Fortunately there was still an architectural hangover from the Georgian period, so it had been designed in better taste than had many of its neighbours.

But Peregrine was not concerned with Windlemere House, which he had seen often enough. He was only hoping that Alstone would not be in one of his disagreeable moods because he was late.

The Duke had an awe-inspiring effect on friend and foe alike and even Peregrine, who was one of his closest friends, found that when he withdrew into an icy reserve to show his disapproval, it was distinctly depressing.

"Mr. Peregrine Gillingham, Your Grace," Dawkins announced at the library door and the Duke, who was reading *The Times*, looked up from the newspaper to say,

"Perry! Why the devil are you so late?"

"I am sorry, Alstone," his friend replied, advancing towards him. "My father sent for me unexpectedly and you know how long-winded he can be."

The Duke threw down the newspaper.

"I suppose I must accept that as an excuse, as I well know that there is no stopping your father once he gets going on a subject that interests him."

"He was not particularly interested in anything," Perry replied ruefully, "only annoyed."

"Money?" the Duke questioned.

"Of course. What else does my father ever talk to me about?"

"You should not be so extravagant!"

"That is all very well for you – " Perry began and then, realising that the Duke was teasing him, he laughed.

"All right, I have been slightly overdoing it lately, but you know as well as I do that Molly is extremely expensive and very much more so since you took an interest in her."

"I did not spoil the market, as you so often tell me I do, for long," the Duke replied.

"Long enough," Perry retorted. "You gave her a taste not only for caviar and champagne but for diamonds too and my allowance from my father has never been able to stretch that far."

He groaned before he added,

"It's hell being a younger son, a situation you have never had to face."

"I also have my difficulties," the Duke pointed out.

"It bewilders me to think what they can possibly be."

As Perry spoke, he accepted a glass of champagne from a silver tray presented to him by a footman.

The Duke also took a glass and then the bottle of champagne, which Dawkins carried, was placed in a magnificent silver wine cooler filled with ice before the two servants withdrew.

"You were telling me about your troubles," the Duke said with a faint smile. "Would you like to listen to mine?"

"I would be delighted, but I have always imagined that you had none."

"Mine are not financial but mental," the Duke replied. "The truth is, Perry, I was thinking before you arrived that I am bored!"

Peregrine sat upright.

"My God, Alstone!" he exclaimed, "if ever I heard a preposterous statement, that is the tallest. You, bored? You, who have everything? I don't believe it."

"It's true," the Duke answered, "and I blame you because by being late you have made me realise it."

"What in God's name have you to be bored about?" Perry asked. "You are the richest man in the British Isles and the biggest landowner, you own the finest and most outstanding horses and you have the pick of every 'fair charmer' in London who takes your fancy!"

He drew in his breath before he continued,

"And we all know the answer to that, it's because you are so *damned* good-looking and the hero of any maiden's dreams!"

"Shut up, Perry, you make me feel sick," the Duke interposed.

"It's nothing to what you make me feel by saying you are bored. Shall I go on with a list of the rest of your possessions? Your yacht, your *Château* in France with the best boar hunting in Europe, your salmon river in Scotland – "

"Keep quiet!" the Duke ordered him. "What I am talking about is something quite different."

"In what way?"

"I think I can best express it as a need for mental stimulation," the Duke said slowly. "The trouble is that everything I do has a certain familiarity about it, which completely eliminates any element of surprise or of anticipation."

He was speaking unexpectedly seriously and his friend looked at him in perplexity.

Perry was in fact quite intelligent when he wanted to be. He realised now that the Duke was not joking or speaking idly but clearly pursuing an unusual and serious train of thought.

"I was thinking last night when we were playing poker," the Duke went on, "that we all knew one another too well for the game to be really amusing. I know immediately when Archie has a good hand because his eyes flicker, Charles's lips tighten when he has a bad one and you click your fingers when you draw to a straight flush."

"*Dammit all*, Alstone, that is almost cheating!" Perry protested.

"Oh the contrary, it is simply being observant and thus knowing for sure what is going to happen, which I may add applies also to my other interests."

"I suppose by that you are referring to Daisy," Perry hazarded. "I have felt for some time that she was beginning to get on your nerves."

He thought for a moment that he had gone too far. The Duke was always very reserved when it came to anybody talking of his love affairs.

But tonight he was in a confiding mood.

"Daisy is without exception the most beautiful woman in London, but even beauty can have a certain sameness about it."

"I agree," Perry replied.

He thought as he spoke that he was not surprised that the Duke was growing bored with the Countess of Hellingford.

There was no doubt about her beauty, which was breathtaking when you first saw her, but she was also inclined to be possessive and at times bossy and, to be honest, he was surprised that the Duke had tolerated her for as long as he had.

"What about a trip abroad?" he asked aloud.

"Where shall I go?" the Duke enquired. "Another thing I was considering last night is that I have visited nearly all the most attractive places in the world, so unless I am prepared to cross the Gobi Desert or climb Mount Everest, there is not much left for me to do."

Perry laughed.

"It really is a case of 'poor little rich boy'!"

"Exactly," the Duke agreed disarmingly. "And so I am asking you for suggestions."

"For Goodness sake, confine your enquiries to me," Perry said. "You know what a furore it would cause if you said anything like this to the Gang. They are very content with things as they are."

The Duke's lips curved in a cynical smile.

He was well aware that what Perry called 'the Gang' was a collection of his friends who depended on him for their racing, fishing, yachting, shooting and every other entertainment that was provided so generously on the Duke's estates and in the many houses he possessed in the countryside.

It had become almost a habit for him to entertain the same people every weekend at Mere, his large and extremely fine house in Surrey.

His special coterie of friends looked on it so much as part of their existence that the same bedrooms were always kept ready for them and they even left a number of their personal possessions behind to save the bother of taking them back to London.

If the Duke intended to change his way of life, Perry thought, there would certainly be weeping and wailing amongst what he secretly called 'hangers-on' and he had no wish to be there to listen to it.

"Where are you thinking of going?" he queried.

"I am not going anywhere, as far as I know," the Duke replied. "I am just asking you what I should do and what I might find interesting instead of sitting waiting as I am now and feeling as if I am becoming fossilised."

"That is the last thing you will ever be," Perry exclaimed. "At the same time I understand what you are saying to me and I shall try to think of a solution."

"All I want is something new, something that is different from the ordinary pattern, that makes my life at the moment seem as dull and unruffled as a duck pond."

"Would you change places with me?" Perry asked. "I can assure you there would be a great deal of ruffle if you had to listen to my father croaking on about responsibility, extravagance and my aimless life that shows that I am nothing but a waster!"

The Duke laughed.

"Your father has always resented your being a friend of mine. He does not think I take my responsibilities seriously enough, as he told my father almost before I was old enough to wear long trousers."

"If he could hear you at the moment, he would realise that you are taking everything far *too* seriously. Enjoy yourself, Alstone! Or why not try marriage? That would certainly be a change!"

There was for a moment an ominous silence.

Then the Duke said,

"You well know the answer to that. Never again! *Never!*"

"That is the most ridiculous statement you have ever made," Perry responded. "Of course you have to marry sometime. What about an heir?"

"My brother, Thomas, has three sons."

"That is not the same as having one yourself. It would amuse you to teach your own boy to ride and shoot and to know that he would carry on the family traditions."

"It is a picture that does not appeal to me in the slightest," the Duke stipulated firmly. "When Elaine was killed, I had no feeling of grief and I can assure you that, having escaped the noose of matrimony once, I have no wish to put the rope round my neck for a second time."

Perry did not answer.

He was remembering that the Duke had been very young when his father arranged for him to marry the daughter of another Duke.

From a social point of view it had been an admirable alliance, but the bride and bridegroom had quarrelled from the moment they had left the Church and, when Alstone's wife was killed while out hunting, everyone expected him to marry again.

From that moment on, however, he made it clear that his intentions where women were concerned were strictly dishonourable.

Surrounded and pursued by the loveliest and most sophisticated women in Society, he chose to amuse himself always with those who were married and had complacent husbands, most of whom were years older than himself.

Only recently, now that he was thirty-three, had the Duke chosen as his companions beauties who were near his own age or younger, but they too were always already married and it is doubtful if he ever met a marriageable girl or spoke to one.

It was the traditional pattern set by the late Monarch, King Edward VII, with the 'Marlborough House Set' at the end of the last century.

Once a beautiful woman had been married for some years and presented her husband with an heir then it was more or less expected that she should enjoy a love affair, provided that it was discreet and never in any way caused a scandal.

King Edward's liaisons, which continued up to the day of his death, were, of course, known to his close friends, but outside the Royal circle, the presence of the beautiful Queen Alexandra on every public occasion protected him even from the newspapers.

Perry was aware that his friend the Duke, while described as a 'lady killer' by his friends, was a paragon of virtue to the outside world.

"Even if you are not at present inclined towards matrimony," he said now, "we shall still have to look round for someone suitable to attract your interest."

"I doubt if you will find anyone," the Duke said gloomily. "I have begun to believe that they are all alike from whatever stratum of Society they may come."

He rose to his feet to walk across the room and poured himself another glass of champagne and, as he did so, he said,

"If you think Molly is extravagant, you have no idea what I am expected to provide."

"You can afford it."

"Yes, but it is decidedly irritating when you know that a woman's real interest in you is that you are a bottomless cornucopia."

The Duke spoke bitterly and Perry laughed as he said,

"I remember an old uncle of mine saying to me once, 'at my age I expect to pay'. By altering the text a little, I can tell you that as a Duke you cannot expect anything for nothing."

The Duke did not reply and Perry went on,

"Stop thinking like an idealist and wanting to be loved for yourself. Just accept what the Gods have given you and be grateful for it. Incidentally, if any of the Gang heard this conversation between us, they would not believe it!"

The Duke chuckled.

"If it will please you, Perry, I will admit that you are right. I am making a fool of myself. We had better go and join the others. I expect they will have arrived by now."

As he spoke, he looked at the clock over the mantelpiece and saw that it was a quarter-to-eight.

"Why do we not go out after dinner?" Perry suggested. "There are masses of parties that I expect we have all been invited to. Or what about seeing the last act at the *Gaiety*?"

"I have already seen it three times," the Duke muttered.

"There are other theatres."

"We are dining too late for that, but if you like we could drop in at *Romano's* later and see if there is anybody there worth looking at."

"All right," Perry agreed, "but I should not mention it in front of Archie and the rest or they will all want to come too."

"No, we will go alone," the Duke promised.

He put down his empty glass and they walked along the lofty passage from the library to the Blue Drawing Room, where the Duke's friends congregated before dinner.

Tonight it was to be a stag party for a number of the guests had come from the races and they wanted to talk about horses, which invariably bored the opposite sex.

There were six men in the Blue Drawing Room and they all had glasses in their hands as the Duke and Perry came into the room.

"Hello, Alstone," they all chorused, lifting their glasses. "We were beginning to think you had forgotten us."

"No, I have not," the Duke replied to them amiably. "Did you have a good day?"

A babble of voices answered him and he learnt that as far as the betting went, it had been a disaster, the favourites having been beaten at the post by outsiders, which nobody had thought to back.

"I am prepared to drown my sorrows," Lord Carnforth said. "But before I do so, I want your opinion, Alstone, on an argument I was having with Hugo when you came into the room."

The Duke took another glass of champagne and, seating himself in a chair, answered,

"I am prepared to adjudicate. What is the subject that you disagree on?"

"We were talking about this new play by George Bernard Shaw," Sir Hugo Benson said. "It's called *Pygmalion*. Have you seen it?"

"No," the Duke replied. "What is it about?"

"It is about a phonetician who trains a flower girl from Covent Garden so cleverly that when she can speak correctly and is well-dressed, he introduces her into Society without anyone being suspicious of her."

"Anything more ridiculous I have never heard!" Lord Carnforth expostulated. "I have rather admired Shaw in the past, because at least he has some interesting ideas, but this is sheer fantasy and an insult to the public's intelligence."

"That is your opinion," Hugo Benson replied. "I say that given a brilliant teacher, a girl young enough to be pliable could possibly, if she had enough intelligence, deceive at any rate a large number of people."

"They would have to be half-witted or morons!" Archie Carnforth exclaimed. "Do you imagine for one moment that any of us could be taken in by an outsider? No, of course not."

"I suppose it might depend on how good-looking the girl was and how well-dressed," Perry suggested.

"We are not talking about prostitutes," Archie Carnforth replied. "We are talking about making a young girl from the gutter deceive intelligent people into believing that she is a Lady of Quality. That is the plot of Shaw's play and I think it's ridiculous!"

"I rather agree with you," one of the other guests remarked. "You know as well as I do that in any Society it is easy to make gaffes that are exceedingly revealing to those in the know."

"What do you mean by that?" someone enquired.

"Well, take a for instance," Archie Carnforth interposed. "Supposing anybody tried to foist some outsider onto us, we would know immediately whether she was genuine or not. It would be like pretending that a paste necklace came from Cartier's. We would recognise it as false at once. What do you think, Alstone?"

"I am inclined to agree with you," the Duke replied. "At the same time I can understand that Shaw's play could be interesting and I must go and see it sometime."

"I should not waste your money," Archie Carnforth said. "The whole thing is rubbish from start to finish!"

"I disagree with you," Hugo Benson said sharply, "for apart from anything else, I think women are so adaptable that like a chameleon they can take their colour from whomever they are with."

"That again is sheer nonsense," Lord Carnforth said aggressively. "Women have to stick, as they always have, to their own environment, to the people with whom they have ties of blood and brain. Outside that they are helpless and they stand out as obviously as a pimple on the nose."

Hugo rose to his feet.

"That is the most damned silly statement I have ever heard!" he boomed. "All through history women have acclimatised themselves and adjusted themselves into Societies that they have been introduced into by circumstances. What is more they have been successful in queening it, literally in some cases, over those who they have associated with,"

"I rather agree with Hugo on that," the Duke remarked.

"I doubt if he can substantiate such a statement," Archie Carnforth said.

"But can *you*?" another man asked.

"Well, look at it this way," Lord Carnforth replied, "we know one another very well and so do the women whom Alstone entertains as he so generously entertains us. Do you imagine that a stranger with an entirely different background, suddenly thrown in amongst us, would not stand out isolated in a most embarrassing manner and be a crashing bore as far as we were concerned?"

"I see what you mean," someone commented, "they would be out of it. They would not understand our jokes or be able to follow the conversation and it might in fact be as embarrassing for us as for them."

"Exactly," Archie continued. "And Hugo can have no answer to that."

"Of course I have an answer," Sir Hugo snapped. "No social set is static. New people enter it, both men and women, and, although at first they may feel slightly strange, they are very quickly absorbed."

"I still say it's not easy, unless they were born into the same social world and have the same interests as those they are associating with," Archie Carnforth retorted.

He looked round the room before he added,

"Can you imagine if we had a man here tonight who had never been racing, never played bridge, not been to a Public School and had never met any of us before? Well, all I can say is that I would feel sorry for the poor devil."

"But suppose he was a woman?" someone asked laughingly.

"Even if she was pretty," Lord Carnforth replied, "or beautiful, if you like, she would still find herself at a loss if she did not know anyone we know and had never been to any of the places we go to and did not appreciate that Alstone is the best-looking Duke in the whole of *Debrett's Peerage*!"

"She would be blind if she did not realise that," Perry said and there was a roar of laughter.

"Where women are concerned it's obviously easier than in the case of a man," Hugo Benson said when the laughter subsided, "and that's why I say that Shaw's contention in *Pygmalion* is perfectly possible."

He paused for a moment and then resumed,

"The Professor took much time and trouble to teach Eliza Doolittle to speak correctly, but after all he was a phonetician. Supposing *we* started with someone who was not born a lady, do you not suppose that very quickly she would feel at home with all of us? And we would accept her without any more questioning?"

"Impossible, completely and absolutely impossible!" Archie Carnforth thundered. "You are talking through your hat, Hugo! Can you see the type of woman you suggest being able to talk to Daisy or Kitty without them seeing through her and having her in tears within ten minutes of her appearance?"

"If she was pretentious, of course," Hugo Benson said. "But if she was very young, like Shaw's Eliza Doolittle, then I think that they would accept her."

"Very young?" Archie Carnforth queried. "Good God, have you ever seen a *debutante* when she first leaves the schoolroom, gauche, inarticulate, hopelessly shy? It always astounds me how the mere act of marriage turns them into the witty charming creatures we all find so alluring."

"I suppose marriage has somewhat the same effect as Shaw's phonetician," Hugo conceded. "Equally we are straying from the point. I am saying that it would be possible to train a complete outsider, like that *damned* horse that won this afternoon, to beat the favourite if it was put into the right race."

The Duke was listening and it was obvious that he was becoming interested in what Sir Hugo was suggesting.

"What you are saying," he said after a moment, "is that if a young girl was introduced into our particular circle, she would not remain gauche and tongue-tied as Archie suggests, but would soon be as polished and assured as we think ourselves to be."

"As indeed we are!" Perry averred.

"Very well. As we are," the Duke accepted.

"That is right," Hugo said. "You have put it very well, Alstone, and what has Archie to say to that?"

"I say you are off your head and such a thing is completely impossible except on the stage. If you are so sure of yourself, Hugo, you had better prove it, as no one will believe you otherwise."

There was a surprised silence.

Then the Duke said in an amused voice,

"That is a challenge, Hugo, and I for one am prepared to put a bet on it!"

"So am I," a man exclaimed. "Who will make a book on it?"

"I will," Perry announced.

He had seen that the idea interested the Duke and he thought it could be an excellent way to rouse him from his introspective mood.

'At least this is something new,' he thought to himself, 'but Heaven knows if we can make it last.'

He walked across the room to an elegant Louis XIV writing table, took a piece of heavily embossed crested writing paper from the velvet box where it was kept and picked up a quill pen.

"Now then, Hugo," he began, "you are not going to rat on us, I hope?"

"I have no intention of doing that," Sir Hugo replied sharply, "but give me a moment to think."

"What we are asking you to do," the Duke said, as if he felt it should all be put clearly, "is to produce a girl, to save time she can be a lady by birth, who has had no contact with the Social world and no experience of anything that is familiar to us. Then in a very short space of time she has to become so much at home in our company that we accept her as one of ourselves. Is that right?"

Hugo Benson nodded.

Lord Carnforth declared with a smile,

"I am prepared to bet one thousand to one that Hugo fails dismally in his extremely speculative aspirations."

"I am prepared to back you in that," the man sitting next to him stated. "All right then, Hugo, I will bet a 'monkey' that the whole experiment fails utterly."

"I accept your bets," Sir Hugo smiled. "What about you, Alstone?"

"I intend to be the Judge," the Duke replied, "and I think we must make it clear from the very beginning, Perry, that the Judge's decision is final."

"Yes, of course," Perry agreed. "Any more bets? I personally intend to support Hugo."

"Thank you, Perry, I have a feeling I shall need a friend."

"You can count on me too," another man came in.

But three other guests bet small sums against Sir Hugo.

"This is going to cost you rather a lot of money," Perry said as he totted it up.

"I am not going to lose," Sir Hugo said, "because, although I swear to you I had not thought of it when this argument started, I think I know exactly the right girl to take part in this experiment."

"We will want to know all about her," the Duke said, "to make quite certain that you are not getting off to an unfair start."

"I am not," Sir Hugo replied, "because I have not seen the girl in question for three years."

"Who is she?"

"She happens to be my niece."

There was silence for a moment and then Lord Carnforth suggested,

"We had better know every detail before we accept Hugo's entry for the contest."

"I am perfectly prepared to give them to you," Hugo Benson answered. "The girl in question is the daughter of my brother, who you may or may not remember was a Parson, the Vicar of a small Parish in Worcestershire."

Someone laughed and then commented,

"Sorry, Hugo, but I had no idea that your brother was a Parson. It is quite the most ludicrous thing I have ever heard that you, the most dashing man-about-town, should have a brother in the Church!"

"It is true," Sir Hugo replied, "and when he died, I sent his daughter to a school in Rome."

"Why did you do that?"

"She seemed a rather artistic, quiet studious girl and I thought she would have a better education there. Also, to be honest, it saved me any worry over holidays."

"You mean," the Duke said perceptively "that Kitty did not know what to do with your niece."

"Exactly," Sir Hugo replied. "Kitty dislikes young girls and has no use for them."

Everyone listening understood only too well that Kitty Benson, who was always engaged in some intense love affair, would certainly not want a young girl in her house, especially one who was unsophisticated and might even be censorious of her aunt's behaviour.

What was more they all realised that Kitty was reaching the age at which she had no wish to be the aunt of anybody.

"So you sent her away to Rome," the Duke said. "What happened then?"

"She has grown up," Sir Hugo replied, "and the school, which incidentally is a kind of Convent, will not keep her any longer."

"A Convent!" Perry exclaimed.

"It is a Convent School," Sir Hugo explained, "where the nuns teach some of the subjects, but there are outside teachers for a number of others. The pupils are predominantly Catholic, but they take girls from other religions and I had no difficulty in arranging for Lorena to go there."

"So Lorena is her name?" the Duke remarked.

Sir Hugo nodded and then turned to the others and said,

"I have been quite frank with you, gentlemen. I have not seen her for three years and she was then, I thought, attractive in a rather unusual way. But anything may have happened in the meantime."

"What you are hoping," someone chipped in, "is that your dark horse will turn out to be a beauty."

"Of course I am hoping that," Sir Hugo agreed. "But I am a sportsman and I hope you realise that I am giving everybody a sporting chance to prove that I am wrong and it will certainly cost me a packet if I am!"

"At least you are right about that," Perry said, looking down at the list in his hand.

"Will you tell us a little more about your niece?" the Duke asked.

"To tell you the truth, I know very little more," Sir Hugo replied. "She has written to me dutifully and they have been quite interesting letters. She is obviously, intelligent and I hope well educated."

"Not *too* well educated – I hope!" a man expostulated. "If there is one thing I really dislike, it is a clever woman!"

"She will have to be clever," Perry objected, "if she is to fulfil all Hugo's hopes of her."

"Yes, of course, I had forgotten that."

"But she may be as stupid, tongue-tied and shy as Archie anticipates," Sir Hugo said. "All I am hoping is that she has a little of the 'chip off the old block' in her and will romp home to a triumphant finish."

"I think you are asking too much," the Duke said with a smile. "But if she is like you, Hugo, she will bowl over Society as apparently Shaw's heroine does."

There was certainly some truth in this for Sir Hugo Benson's name was a byword of smartness and *savoir faire*.

He was in some ways the modern equivalent of the Georgian dandies and bucks who had centred round the Prince Regent.

King Edward had found him one of the most amusing of his friends and a party seldom took place at Marlborough House, and subsequently at

Buckingham Palace, without Sir Hugo being in attendance.

When the King died, Sir Hugo had attached himself to the Duke and enlivened what was known as the Windlemere Set, bringing his wit, his sense of humour and his originality to those who tried to keep the Duke as their special property.

He was now well over forty, but he looked much younger and his good figure and the smartness of his dress was the envy of every ambitious young man in the Social world.

It was so like Hugo to suggest some new amusement, Perry thought, as they walked into dinner and he told himself that for the moment this was the answer to the Duke's cry for something new.

There was no doubt that the Duke was interested because, as he sat down at the head of the table, with Sir Hugo on his right, he asked,

"When does our experiment start?"

"That is what I want to know," Lord Carnforth said. "And there is to be no cheating, Hugo, in that you coach the girl beforehand."

"Do you mean that?" Sir Hugo enquired. "If I cannot talk to her and tell her what is expected, it will be a very severe handicap as far as I am concerned."

"I think she needs a handicap because she is your niece," someone piped up and laughed.

"As adjudicator, I cannot allow Hugo to have to carry too much weight," the Duke added.

"I can see that Archie is really suspicious of me," Sir Hugo said, "so I am prepared to take a chance. Which you certainly should appreciate."

"What is that?" Lord Carnforth asked.

"I will allow anyone you choose to come with me to meet Lorena when she arrives the day after tomorrow at Victoria Station. Then it will be up to you to decide where we take her and how you all meet her for the first time."

There was silence for a moment and then the Duke said,

"I was going to suggest that she comes here, but the day after tomorrow is Friday and I had intended to go down to Mere."

"Of course," Archie Carnforth exclaimed. "Mere would be the perfect place to try out her paces."

"I think," Sir Hugo said with a smile, "she will find Mere so overwhelming and so grandiose that she will be stricken dumb the moment she sees it."

"Can you think of somewhere better to go?" Archie asked.

"No and once again, I accept the challenge," Sir Hugo said. "Alstone is right. A party at Mere would be a severe test for any woman let alone an inexperienced girl and will prove my point once and for all."

"Personally I think you are crazy, even though I am supporting you," Perry said. "But if you pick up your niece at Victoria Station, you can then drive in one of Alstone's cars to Mere in an hour and a half."

"I agree," Sir Hugo nodded, "and you can send anybody you like, Archie, to accompany us so that you shall know that I am not doping the horse before the race begins!"

"I will consider who it should be," Archie Carnforth replied.

"Take your time," Sir Hugo said good-humouredly. "We should arrive at Mere at about six o'clock and give the child time to change for dinner."

He looked round the table with a smile that seemed to be one of self-satisfaction.

'He is betting on a certainty,' Perry thought to himself, 'or else he is more of a reckless gambler than even I imagined.'

However he was not particularly concerned about Sir Hugo, for he was thinking that for the moment at any rate the boredom had vanished from the Duke's eyes.

*

As the train reached the outskirts of London, Lorena began to collect her luggage and the two other girls in the carriage with her did the same.

The Sister, who had accompanied them all the way from Rome, said sharply in broken English,

"Now, *mesdemoiselles*, don't leave anything behind. You don't want to lose your possessions."

"No, indeed, *madame*," one of the girls replied, "although, of course, my mother has some wonderful gowns waiting for me and especially the one I am to wear at my Presentation."

"I wonder whether we shall be presented in the same drawing room," the other girl reflected. "What about you, Lorena?"

"I don't know what will happen to me," Lorena answered in a soft voice. "You see, I have no mother to present me. In fact both my parents are dead."

"I had forgotten that you are an orphan!" one of the girls exclaimed. "Oh, poor Lorena! But perhaps I shall be able to see you if you are in London."

"Again I have no idea where I shall be," Lorena replied. "My uncle only writes to me occasionally and tells me very little news. It is rather frightening stepping into a new life and having no idea what it will be like or even where I shall be living."

"It sounds horrid to me," one of her friends then remarked, "but I expect you will be all right. You are too clever to be anything else."

"I wish that was true," Lorena smiled, "but I know that my aunt at any rate is not going to be very impressed by book learning."

As she spoke, she thought of her Aunt Kitty as she had last seen her, exquisitely dressed but with what Lorena thought was a hard expression on her pretty face.

Lorena had asked her quite innocently if she would be allowed to come home from Rome in the holidays.

"Come home?" Lady Benson had said in a hard voice. "If by home you mean here, the answer is 'no'! You will stay in Rome until you are fully educated and that will take at least the next three years."

"All that – time?" Lorena had asked in dismay.

"You are a very lucky girl," Lady Benson had said. "It costs your uncle a great deal of money to send you to Rome. You will have an excellent education, far better, I am sure, than your father would ever have been able to afford. You might at least be grateful."

"I am very, very grateful," Lorena had replied. "It is just the idea of being with – strangers and of – knowing nobody."

"As you are an orphan, you have to get used to strangers as you call them," Lady Benson had said. "And let me make it quite clear, Lorena, that I have no time and certainly no inclination to chaperone a young girl. I don't like children and have none of my own, thank Goodness!"

"I – understand," Lorena had replied humbly.

When she had left her uncle's house the next morning to travel with some other girls who were going to Rome, she had not been able to say 'goodbye' to her aunt because she had not yet been called.

Uncle Hugo had always been very kind to her, but she found him rather frightening.

He was so unlike her father in every way and it was strange to think that they were brothers.

She had learnt when she was quite young that her father had chosen to go into the Church in the teeth of opposition from his father and from his elder brother.

He had heard a call to help other people to worship God as he did and no argument would make him join the family Regiment as had been intended.

When still a Curate he had married the daughter of a country Squire who was as unworldly as himself, but they loved each other in a way that made anywhere they lived seem to have an aura of happiness that no money could buy.

After they were both dead, Lorena knew that her special world, which had always seemed to be filled with sunshine, music and laughter, had gone forever.

It had taken her some time to adjust herself to school life and not even the nuns had realised how much she suffered or how homesick she was for a home that was no longer there and how she longed for her mother and father, who were together in a place that she could not reach.

They thought her very quiet.

Then the sweetness of her nature, her understanding of other people's problems and her most unusual perceptiveness, which made her different from other girls, gradually made those who at first had barely noticed her aware that she was not only there but important to them personally.

Anyone in trouble turned to Lorena instinctively.

She listened to the worries not only of the girls of her own age but also of everyone else in the Convent, the visiting teachers, the Italian servants, who were always ready to talk, and even the nuns themselves.

She had a capacity for listening and, although she might say little, she made those she listened to feel that they had found a solution to their problem.

It was largely because she made them find within themselves the answers they needed, a quality and a virtue that finally commended itself to the Mother Superior.

"It has been a happiness for all of us to have you here," she told Lorena when she said 'goodbye'. "You have developed a great deal for which I hope we can take some credit, but I think actually what you have, my child, is something that God gives us at birth and we either develop it or are not aware of its existence."

Lorena smiled.

"I hope I have – developed, Reverend Mother."

"You have and it is a virtue that will stand you in good stead now that you are going out into the world. I understand that you are not yet certain where you will live or who will look after you."

"I am – sure that my uncle will find – someone," Lorena said hesitatingly.

The Reverend Mother knew that she was feeling apprehensive.

"You must trust in God," she told her, "and always remember, my child, to use your instinct. It will tell you what is right and what is wrong and it is the way that God speaks to us, especially if we need His guidance."

"I shall remember, Reverend Mother," Lorena said.

During the long journey across France, she thought over what had been said.

She knew in her heart that her instincts would have to help her in a great number of ways that perhaps the Reverend Mother did not envisage.

There was nothing in the books she had read at the Convent to tell her anything of the Social world that she knew her uncle belonged to and in which she had no doubt that her aunt would not wish her to play any part.

Her father had often laughed about his brother's important place in Society and the way he associated with Royalty as if it was his right.

"How I should have hated it!" Lorena had heard him say often enough.

"It must be very interesting, Papa," she had hazarded.

"It depends on what you want out of life," her father replied. "The superficial trappings of pomp and circumstance certainly are not for me. But if they make my brother Hugo happy, I am the last person to tell him that he should seek anything different."

"It must be fascinating to know the King and the beautiful Queen Alexandra," Lorena had commented.

"There is a great deal of glamour about them," her father had conceded. "At the same time they are people, just like old Mr. and Mrs. Briggs, who I am calling on now because they will be celebrating their Golden Wedding Anniversary next week."

He smiled before he added,

"Not that there will be much gold about it, but I am sure your mother is prepared to bake them a cake."

"Of course, dearest," her mother replied. "I have already planned it, and as I do not think the icing would look very pretty in yellow, have bought some golden candles to put on top of it."

"You think of everything, darling," her husband had said.

He kissed her before he left the Vicarage.

'They were so very happy,' Lorena now thought to herself.

She wondered if Uncle Hugo could possibly be happy in the same way with Aunt Kitty, who had said that she 'had no children, thank Goodness'.

Her father and mother had always deeply regretted that they had had only one child.

"I would like to have had a dozen children as they would have made your father so happy," her mother had said once. "But God had other ideas and, after you were born, the doctors told me that I could have no more."

"How can I make up to you for all the children you have not had?" Lorena asked her.

Her mother put her arms round her and held her close.

"You have done that already," she said. "Daddy and I are perfectly content to have one adorable daughter and a very pretty one at that."

"I shall never be as pretty as you. Mummy."

"It is fun to be pretty," her mother had replied, "but it is wonderful when the man you love thinks you are beautiful."

"That is what Daddy thinks."

"Yes, I know," her mother had answered, "and that is why I am not only the luckiest woman in the world but also the happiest."

'That is what I want in my life,' Lorena thought as the train carried her towards London, 'to be as happy as Mummy and Daddy were.'

She was still thinking of them when the train drew slowly along the platform at Victoria Station.

She then saw her Uncle Hugo, looking most elegant, his top hat on his head and a carnation in his buttonhole, waiting on the platform with another gentleman beside him.

CHAPTER TWO

Waiting on the platform, Sir Hugo admitted to himself that he was apprehensive.

He had not really meant to become so involved in a wager that might easily cost him a great deal of money.

He had had too much to drink at the races and, although he was never drunk, he was far too fastidious for that, he thought afterwards that it must have slightly distorted his usual common sense.

The real reason that he had entered into the argument was that Archie Carnforth had annoyed him.

He was in fact the only close friend of the Duke's who Sir Hugo had little liking for.

He was so self-opinionated, so absolutely certain that he was always right and that his opponents on whatever subject must therefore of necessity be wrong.

He had been particularly irritating at the races where, when each one of the outsiders won, he lectured the rest of the party on how they should have been knowledgeable enough to have anticipated that a particular horse had a chance.

Although he was a well-known racehorse owner, he seldom placed a bet and Hugo Benson and a number of other people found that in itself distinctly tiresome.

Anyway, Sir Hugo thought, he had let himself in for what promised to be a difficult and uncomfortable visit to Mere and instead of looking forward, as he usually did, to being with the Duke and his friends, he was definitely feeling anxious.

Too late he thought that he should have insisted on keeping Lorena for a week in London so that he could at least dress her suitably before he presented her to his opponents in the contest.

That was what Professor Higgins in *Pygmalion* had done and Sir Hugo thought that he had been singularly remiss in forgetting that the clothes a woman was dressed in were perhaps more important than anything else.

'I have made a fool of myself,' he reflected ruefully.

And, as if he sensed what he was feeling, Perry, who was with him, urged,

"Cheer up, Hugo. Your traditional good luck will stand you in good stead."

Sir Hugo laughed.

"Is it so obvious that I am anticipating the worst?"

"You have spoken barely a word since we left *White's Club*," Perry replied, "and that is unusual to say the least of it."

Over dinner at Mere they had had quite a fight as to who should actually accompany Sir Hugo to the Railway Station.

Lord Carnforth had suggested that he himself should go, but that had been turned down because, as

Hugo Benson said, he was so deeply involved that he might easily contrive in one way or another to make Lorena nervous and wary of what was waiting for her.

Finally the Duke decided who it was to be, saying that as Judge he was appointing Perry, believing that he could rely on him to be impartial as it was a question of sportsmanship.

"He may be supporting you, Hugo," the Duke said, "but he will feel responsible to me in seeing that you take no unfair advantage on the way to Mere."

"If you ask me, I am carrying far too much weight in this race," Sir Hugo complained. "Firstly I am not allowed to warn the child, secondly, she will have a stranger in the shape of Perry listening to every word she says and thirdly she will already be feeling tired after journeying all the way from Rome."

"I will take all those facts into consideration," Lord Carnforth said in a manner that set Sir Hugo's teeth on edge.

Now Sir Hugo turned to Perry,

"I have just realised that I should at least have been allowed to dress Lorena for the part she is to play."

"That is the wrong expression," Perry said quickly. "She is not allowed to know that it is a part. If she puts on an act, you know as well as I do that it will be obvious to everybody."

Sir Hugo nodded.

"At the same time she will, I suppose, be wearing only the clothes she has worn at school,"

He groaned as he thought how badly dressed the schoolgirls were he had sometimes seen parading crocodile fashion through Hyde Park.

If Lorena looked anything like them, he decided that he would call the whole thing off and refuse to take her to Mere.

"I am not going to make a laughing stock of myself," he said aloud.

There was a look of surprise on Perry's face and Sir Hugo explained,

"I am aware that I made a vital error from the word 'go'. Let's make it quite clear, Perry, that if the child is plain, spotty and badly dressed, you go to Mere without me. I am not going to have Archie crowing over me from the moment he sees her and every time she opens her mouth."

"I see no reason why she should not be attractive if she is your niece," Perry pointed out disarmingly.

"Archie is right," Sir Hugo continued gloomily, "unfledged girls of that age are gauche, stupid and shy. Why the devil did I get into this mess in the first place?"

"Because it annoyed you that Archie was so dogmatic."

Sir Hugo laughed.

"That is true," he admitted.

"Well, I am interested in this competition or whatever you like to call it," Perry said, "not only because I agree with you as Archie can be infuriatingly dictatorial, but also because it appears to amuse Alstone."

Sir Hugo smiled.

"I imagined that was why you were supporting me."

"He is bored, Hugo. It seems incredible, but he is!"

"That is Daisy's fault," Sir Hugo replied. "She has been presuming on his affections for far too long. I could have warned her that he was chafing at the bit."

"Why did you not do so?"

Sir Hugo grinned.

"Daisy has done her best on several occasions to 'put a spoke in my wheel'."

"So it was 'tit-for-tat'!"

"Exactly. I am hoping that once Alstone is free of her, he will find a woman who is more amenable and certainly one who is more pleasant to his friends."

"Have you anyone in mind?" Perry enquired.

"As a matter of fact there is someone," Sir Hugo answered, "who I nearly suggested might be invited to Mere this week until I thought that it might confuse the issue."

"Yes, of course. We want Alstone to concentrate on the contest. She had better come another time and certainly not when Daisy is there."

"That is what I thought," Sir Hugo agreed. "As Daisy is to be at Mere this week, there is no room for anyone else."

The two men smiled knowingly at each other.

The Countess of Hellingford had been overbearing and, they thought, at times disloyal to both of them.

Because they were genuinely fond of the Duke, they felt it essential to protect him from anyone who exploited him too obviously and that was particularly true of women.

Because he was so rich, those he favoured invariably took advantage of his generosity, which was indeed understandable up to a certain point.

But Daisy Hellingford was greedy and it was not only the diamonds she wore round her neck that the Duke had paid for but the horses she rode and the cars she was driven in.

She also expected him to provide a great many other things that were not usually in the category of permissible gifts from a man to his mistress.

Daisy was by no means impoverished and her husband, who was conveniently big game hunting in Africa, was decently well off and owned a large estate in Gloucestershire.

That he was not travelling without female companionship enabled Daisy to gain the sympathy of women in playing the part of a wronged wife.

But Sir Hugo and Perry were convinced that, if there was anything irregular about the whole arrangement, it was of Daisy's doing.

"I can tell you one thing," Perry said now, "when they do part, we will make *damned* sure that someone at Mere counts the Van Dykes and the collection of snuffboxes."

Sir Hugo laughed.

They were both thinking of another of the Duke's ladyloves he had parted from with much recrimination on her side only to find after the break was final that quite a number of the miniatures, which were family heirlooms, had mysteriously disappeared.

They had been returned after quite a large amount of money had changed hands in compensation.

"Here comes the train," Sir Hugo now exclaimed.

Perry thought with slight amusement that his friend was definitely tense and it was so amazingly unlike Sir Hugo to be worried about anything.

He was one of those people who always seem to be riding high and immune from the small and irrelevant anxieties of the common herd, so this was certainly an unusual condition for him to be in.

The train puffed slowly to the end of the platform and Perry found that he too was intensely curious as to what Lorena would look like.

It would certainly be great fun and a triumph if she was as attractive as he and her uncle hoped, but his common sense told him that this was very unlikely.

She might not be quite as bad as Archie Carnforth depicted, but he was right in saying that a schoolgirl, any schoolgirl, would be out of place at Mere with the men and women who were among the most sophisticated to be found in Europe.

Now that King Edward was dead and the hostesses who had presided over the brilliant and glittering salons that had been so much a part of his reign had gone, there was only the Windlemere Set left to glitter with what was not only a social but also an intellectual brilliance.

The women were chosen for their beauty and the men for their brains.

Like Sir Hugo Perry was wondering how they could ever have become involved in such an absurd idea as to imagine that they could perform their own version of *Pygmalion* amongst themselves.

'It's all that *damned* fellow Bernard Shaw's fault,' he thought. 'I believe he has been a troublemaker all his life in one way or another.'

As the passengers were pouring out of the train, Sir Hugo stood watching them, leaning lightly on his Malacca cane, with his polished top hat at an angle on his head and looking completely at his ease.

Only Perry knew that what he was feeling was very different.

Then Sir Hugo uttered almost beneath his breath,

"Here she is!"

Perry turned his head to see a girl approaching them.

For a moment he thought that she was far too young to be Lorena, who he knew was eighteen and then, as she drew nearer, he was sure of it.

But she had seen Sir Hugo and was now running towards him with a little cry.

"Uncle Hugo!" she exclaimed, a lilt in her voice. "I was hoping you would come to meet me. It's so lovely to see you and delightful to be home again."

Sir Hugo kissed her cheek and then said,

"I am glad to have you back, Lorena. Let me look at you, you don't appear to have grown very much."

He held her from him at arm's length and Perry knew that he had another reason for inspecting her, besides the fact that she was his niece.

Then, as he looked at her closely, Perry drew in his breath.

If he had hoped for something different from the ordinary schoolgirl, his hopes had certainly been fulfilled.

Lorena was not in the slightest like any schoolgirl he had ever seen before.

Looking at her face it was difficult to believe that she could be more than fifteen or sixteen, but her body beneath the blue travelling gown she wore was sweetly curved.

But for the moment Perry was concerned only with her face and it was not difficult to realise that she was in fact not pretty but lovely, yet in a different way from other women.

It was the fashion, as it had been from the beginning of the century, for the beauties who were most admired to be tall, fair and blue-eyed and somewhat Junoesque as regards their figures.

Lorena was none of these things.

She was small, slim and had the pale fairness of a dawn sky, while her eyes were the transparent blue of a thrush's egg.

Because she looked so young, her face should have been round, but instead her chin was pointed, her small nose was very straight and her lips curved.

'She reminds me of something,' Perry thought, 'but I cannot put a name to it.'

Then, as Sir Hugo introduced him and she smiled, he felt as if she held the sunshine in her strange eyes and her smile was a spontaneous delight that somehow reminded him of his childhood.

"This is Peregrine Gillingham," Sir Hugo was saying, "an old friend of mine who is accompanying us on the journey we are now taking to the country."

"To the country, Uncle Hugo!" Lorena exclaimed. "How wonderful! Where are we going?"

"To stay with another friend of mine, the Duke of Windlemere," Sir Hugo answered, "at his house, which is one of the finest in England. I think you will enjoy seeing it."

"It sounds very exciting," Lorena smiled. "But more exciting than anything else is to be with you."

The porters found Lorena's luggage, which Perry noticed consisted only of two small leather trunks and they went slowly along the platform, Lorena apologising that the train was late owing to the fact that they had had a rough crossing of the English Channel.

"Were you seasick?" Sir Hugo enquired.

"No, but a great many other people were," Lorena replied. "I was so sorry for them, but there was nothing I could do, so I stayed up on deck."

"That sounds very sensible," Sir Hugo approved.

They walked out of the Station and found waiting outside two large very impressive cars. The first was driven by a chauffeur in dark green uniform and beside him was a footman wearing the Windlemere livery.

The other car behind it was for the luggage and it also carried Sir Hugo's and Perry's valets.

Lorena stepped into the first car and, as she seated herself on the back seat, she enthused,

"This too is very exciting. I have only ridden in a car three or four times since I left England."

"Are you telling me there are no cars in Rome?" Perry asked.

"Oh, no, there are plenty of them," Lorena replied, "but the nuns expected us to walk everywhere and I only went in a car when one of the other pupils invited me out. But most people in Rome prefer to drive in open carriages. It is so much easier to see the beauty of the City when you are not going too fast."

"I am sure that is true," Perry commented, "and, when we go tearing about the countryside at a hundred miles an hour, we shall see nothing but our own dust and hear nothing but the roar of engines!"

"I prefer horses," Sir Hugo said, "but it is certainly far quicker to travel as we are now and, although the train was late, we shall still have time to change for dinner without rushing."

As if changing for dinner made him think of Lorena's clothes again, he turned to his niece to say,

"I hope you have something attractive to wear. This will be a very smart party."

She did not answer for a moment and Perry had the distinct idea that Sir Hugo was holding his breath.

"I think," Lorena replied, "that the clothes I bought in Rome with the money you so kindly sent me every year are attractive, but perhaps they will not be smart enough – for your friends."

As she spoke, she remembered how her father had always described his brother's friends as being rich and smart and how he had laughed about their 'superficial trappings of pomp and circumstance.'

There was suddenly a worried look in her blue eyes and as, if Sir Hugo could not bear to make her anxious of what lay ahead or to feel self-conscious, he said quickly,

"I am certain that you have good taste and I like what you are wearing now."

It was, Perry thought, a very simple get-up, but in some way that he could not explain it was completely right on Lorena, just as her travelling hat suited her as it turned back from her face and gave her the little girl look that he had noticed the moment he saw her.

The fashion was for large hats copiously decorated with feathers and flowers, but Lorena's hat was trimmed only with blue ribbons and looked rather like a halo as it circled her small head.

The cars were soon clear of London and Lorena leant forward to watch the countryside as they passed through it.

"I had forgotten that England is so green," she said, almost as if she was speaking to herself, "and the trees are beautiful. I know now how much – I have missed it all these last three years."

"Have you been homesick?" Sir Hugo enquired.

"I think that is the right word," Lorena answered, "even though I no longer have a home but perhaps one naturally longs for one's own environment and for the land that one belongs to by birth."

Perry was startled.

She was saying in different words what Archie Carnforth had averred about environment. Hers had been a Vicarage in the country and that was as far removed from Mere as the North Pole from the South Pole.

As the cars seemed to eat up the miles swiftly and smoothly, Perry noticed that Lorena did not chatter as most other women would have done. He was sure that Sir Hugo appreciated the fact that she was quiet.

It was always a bore to talk above the noise of a car, but he wondered if Lorena was silent because she had nothing to say or if she was sensitive enough to realise that men did not wish to talk in such circumstances.

They had almost reached Mere before Sir Hugo said,

"I think I ought to tell you to expect quite a large party, who are all close friends of the Duke and I know that you will be sorry that your aunt cannot be here this week as she has to visit her mother who is ill."

"Oh, poor Aunt Kitty. I am sorry," Lorena said.

Even as she spoke she felt that it was wrong of her to feel relieved.

She had not forgotten the way that her aunt had spoken to her before she had been sent off to Rome.

She had said then that she had no wish to chaperone a young girl and doubtless she had not changed her mind.

It had made Lorena worry about what was to happen to her and where she would be sent when she reached England, but it was a joy to know that she would have a week alone with her uncle wherever they might be staying.

Although they had been so different in temperament, he was her beloved father's brother and there was now, although Sir Hugo would not have agreed, a resemblance that Lorena could see even if no one else would have been able to do so.

It was, she thought, in the way he smiled, the way he spoke and sometimes in the expression in his eyes.

But her father had not been smart in that he did not dress with the meticulous elegance that she had always known was characteristic of her uncle.

Nevertheless, because they were brothers, there was a family resemblance that made her feel that she had come home and that some part of her family, if only a small part, was waiting for her.

"I shall like meeting your friends, Uncle Hugo," she ventured, "and will you please tell me if I do anything wrong? I would not want you to be ashamed of me."

"I am quite certain I shall not be," Sir Hugo replied. "What I am going to suggest is that, as soon as we arrive, you go up to your room and take your time in changing into your very best gown. First appearances are always important."

Lorena laughed.

"Now you are making me nervous, although I am quite certain that no one will even notice me. But I want to look at all the interesting and fun people that you know. Mama sometimes used to read their names out of *The Court Circular* and it always sounded to me like listening to a Fairytale."

The way she spoke was so simple and natural that Perry said,

"You are quite right, Lorena, that is just what it is and, when you see the Duke, you will know that he is

Prince Charming, although your uncle is a good runner-up for that role."

"You flatter me," Sir Hugo laughed.

Lorena clapped her hands together.

"What you are saying is that like Cinderella I am going to a ball and what could be a better coach than the one we are travelling in? Although, of course, it ought to have six white ponies to pull it!"

"In which case," Perry replied, "we should not only miss the Prince's banquet but it would be after midnight before we arrived."

Lorena laughed with delight.

"That would be too disappointing and I would not even have a glass slipper to leave behind. Not that I have a pair to wear this evening!"

"Never mind," Sir Hugo said. "Make yourself look as pretty as possible and I will come and collect you when it is time to go downstairs to dinner."

"Thank you, Uncle Hugo. It is so kind of you and I promise I will not keep you waiting."

"You had better not," Perry said. "The Duke is very punctilious about time and, if there is one thing that makes him angry, it is people being late for dinner."

The way he spoke made Lorena look at him reflectively and then he asked her,

"What are you thinking?"

"You sound almost as if you are afraid of the Duke," she answered frankly. "Perhaps after all he is not Prince Charming but the Demon King!"

Both Perry and Sir Hugo chuckled,

"Wait until you see him," Perry advised her after a moment. "You will not say that then."

Lorena thought Mere indeed looked like a Fairy Palace from the first moment she saw it.

The huge roof surmounted by the Duke's standard was silhouetted against the sky and she stared wide-eyed at the largest and most famous Robert Adam mansion in the whole of Great Britain.

Its huge dome, the wings springing out from the centre building, its Corinthian column entrance and the hundreds of windows gleaming golden in the setting sun were not only gloriously beautiful but also so impressive that Lorena told herself that this was the England that she had always wanted to see.

Her father might have disparaged the life that his brother lived, but she had felt that it had a glamour and a mystique about it that stimulated her imagination and even coloured her dreams.

Now for the first time she would see for herself the England that had made the eighteenth century a time of notable architectural development, the England that in the reign of King George IV had set a standard of luxury and elegance which was the envy of all Europe.

Because that was a period of history that Lorena most enjoyed, she had hoped almost against hope that the England which had become even more prosperous in Queen Victoria's time had not changed too drastically after her death.

There had been few books in the school library to describe to her the history of England since the beginning of the century and she had been afraid that by the time she returned home she would find that the grandeur and splendour had passed with the death of King Edward VII.

Even at the Convent she had heard talk of its being 'the end of an era' and that King George and Queen Mary were very different from the flamboyant Monarch who had been called the 'Uncle of Europe'.

But here, right in front of her eyes, was the splendour and glory that she so longed to see.

When they entered the huge marble hall with statues of Gods and Goddesses set in niches in the walls, Lorena stared round her with delight.

The footmen with their powdered wigs and knee breeches were exactly what she had expected and, when on her uncle's instructions, she was escorted up the huge carved staircase to where a housekeeper in rustling black silk with a silver chatelaine falling from her waist was waiting for her, Lorena wanted to exclaim with joy that it was everything that she had hoped for.

"Will you come this way, miss?" the housekeeper was saying. "I'll take you to your bedroom, which, as I thought you'd wish, is close to your uncle's."

"It is so kind of you to think of it," Lorena replied.

Then, as if she could not help herself, she exclaimed,

"What a wonderful house this is!"

"I'm glad you should think so, miss."

"And how long have you been here?" Lorena enquired. "I am afraid I did not hear your name. Perhaps you would tell it to me."

"Mrs. Kingston, miss. I'm called 'Mrs', although I've never been married."

"I expect you look on this house as your home," Lorena said and the housekeeper smiled at her.

"That be true, miss. We all of us who have been here many years feel as if Mere belongs to us as well as to His Grace. But then, as almost everyone employed here was born on the estate, it's very much a family business, so to speak."

She laughed a little at her own joke and Lorena remarked,

"How comforting that sounds and you would miss it very much if it was not here, just as I miss my home and my family."

"I understand your parents are dead, miss," Mrs. Kingston said. "It's ever so sad for you, but I feel sure Sir Hugo will look after you. We're all very fond of him here at Mere."

As she spoke, she showed Lorena into a bedroom that made her exclaim with delight again.

There was a four-poster bed with chintz curtains, a dressing table with a muslin flounce round it and

Lorena saw that the room contained all the little luxuries that one of the girls at school had told her were to be found in all large houses that entertained in the proper way.

"You would be surprised, Lorena," she had said, "at the number of things Mama believes are essential to comfort, lots of little satin cushions covered with lace, a writing table where there are no less than twenty different items that must be supplied in case a guest wishes to write a letter."

"What can they all be?" Lorena had asked.

"A leather blotter, a box to match to hold writing paper, a silver inkstand, a pen holder, a little pin cushion, a letter opener, a calendar, framed lists of the times the posts leave, a pen tray, a notebook and lots, lots more that I cannot remember," her friend reeled off.

She took a breath and continued,

"Then, of course, there must be flowers in the bedroom, carnations or lilies, or orchids if the guest is very grand."

Lorena had laughed at the idea of flowers being chosen according to one's social status.

She noticed that there were lilies in her room and wondered if they were one step up from roses or perhaps a step below carnations.

She was nearly ready for dinner when there was a knock on the door and the maid who was helping her to dress opened it.

She brought in a tray on which were arranged a number of corsages of different varieties of flowers.

"Will you choose, miss, which you would like to wear?" she asked.

"What a lovely idea!" Lorena exclaimed. "Do all the Duke's guests have a choice like this?"

"Yes, of course, miss," the maid replied, "and the gentlemen are offered carnations or gardenias for buttonholes."

Lorena found herself hesitating between a corsage of gardenias and another of small star-shaped orchids.

"Which shall I choose?" she asked the maid.

"I thinks the orchids, miss, If you like, I'll arrange them in your hair."

"What a good idea," Lorena smiled. "And thank you for helping me."

As she had no jewellery, she thought that the orchids were very decorative and she hoped that her uncle would think they made her look smarter than she would have looked without them.

Her best evening gown was one that had been made for her by a dressmaker in Rome whom she preferred to those patronised by the other girls of her age.

Her uncle had given her quite a generous allowance to spend, a gesture, although she did not know it, to placate his conscience when she wrote a little wistfully that most of the girls were going home for the holidays while she was to stay at school.

Because Lorena loved the beautiful paintings that she could see in Rome and appreciated the drapery of the ancient statuary, she preferred almost classical clothes to the more elaborate and fussy creations that were in vogue.

When she looked at the statues of Goddesses, Greek and Roman that were to be seen everywhere, she felt that nothing could be more beautiful and they appealed to her senses in a way that she found hard to describe because to look at them was somehow an emotional experience.

So Lorena chose to have her gowns made in white or pure colours and to adapt the fashion so that there was something classical in every line, in every draped bodice and softly falling skirt.

Now when she looked at herself in the mirror wearing a white gown, she wondered if she had been right and if her uncle would be disappointed in her.

"You look very lovely, if I may say so, miss," the maid commented.

"Thank you," Lorena replied. "I am just hoping that I will not look out of place in the grandeur of this magnificent house."

Then she gave a little laugh.

"There is one consolation, nobody is likely to notice me when there are so many other things to look at!"

The maid had no time to reply for at that moment Sir Hugo knocked on the door.

"May I come in?" he enquired.

"Yes, of course, Uncle Hugo, I am quite ready."

She ran towards him and, when he saw the white orchids in her hair, he smiled.

"I have been wondering which flowers you would choose," he said.

"It was quite a difficult choice," Lorena replied, "but Emily has helped me. She has been very kind in looking after me, Uncle Hugo."

"I am glad about that."

He then nodded to the maid, who bobbed him a respectful curtsey as he and Lorena left the room.

"Is there anybody I ought to greet in a different way from the others?" Lorena asked as she and Sir Hugo walked down the stairs.

"What do you mean by that?" he enquired.

"I know that one curtseys to Royalty," Lorena replied, "and when a Cardinal came to the Convent we all had to genuflect and kiss his ring."

Sir Hugo smiled.

"I promise you that there will be no Cardinals here tonight nor, as it happens, is there anyone of Royal blood, although it is quite a frequent occurrence for the Duke to have either a member of our Royal Family or one from another country staying in his house."

"If I meet a Royal Prince, it will make it more like a Fairy story than ever!" Lorena enthused.

"Wait until you see the Duke," Sir Hugo replied.

He entered the Blue Drawing Room and, as he did so, he was conscious that there was a sudden hush amongst the crowd of people congregated at the far end of the room.

With the artistry of a showman he had deliberately waited until he thought that the majority of the guests would be downstairs before he brought Lorena in to meet them.

He was not quite certain what they would think of her unusual appearance and her gown had certainly surprised him. At the same time he had known from years of experience that there was a rightness about it that could not have been improved upon by Frederic Worth himself.

The softly draped bodice, the small waist with its wide sash and the skirt caught up in the front so that it fell into classical folds below her slim hips were a perfect frame for the delicacy of her face and features and the translucent whiteness of her skin.

Whether it was by design or by chance, the only touch of colour about Lorena was the strange blue of her eyes and there was a faint smile of triumph on Sir Hugo's lips as they walked towards their host.

He knew that every man in the room was staring at Lorena critically.

The women, who had not been let into the secret of the wager, were interested in her as a new arrival only because she was his niece.

He had deliberately asked the Duke not to pay Lorena more attention than he would ordinarily have given to any new arrival.

"If you make the child seem of the least interest," he had said, "you know as well as I do that the women will be down on her like a ton of bricks."

"I will try to ensure you are not handicapped in that way at any rate," the Duke remarked.

"In this instance I am not worrying about myself so much as about Lorena," Sir Hugo replied. "Kitty has already insisted that I find a relative of some sort to take her off our hands and quite frankly her time at Mere will decide which one, although as it happens, the choice is not wide."

"I never would have thought of finding you short of anything, least of all relations," the Duke declared with a laugh.

"I have plenty of them, but they are either too old, too impoverished or too egotistical to want to be encumbered with a young girl."

"That last objection might apply to you yourself," the Duke replied, "and if you want the truth, I think it is rather selfish of Kitty not to give the child a chance."

"That is exactly what I said," Sir Hugo agreed. "I thought we would keep her for a Season and try to get her married off, but Kitty has refused categorically."

There was a note in Sir Hugo's voice that told the Duke that it had been a bone of contention between them.

'It's a pity,' he had thought, 'that Hugo has no children of his own.'

He was the sort of man who would have liked to have a son at Eton who would follow in his footsteps by serving in the Life Guards.

Then he remembered that people might think the same about himself and determined not to pursue the subject.

"Let's hope," he said now, "that your niece's first taste of caviar and champagne does not make it very difficult for her later to settle down to tea and buns or whatever your relations are prepared to offer her."

"That is exactly what it will be," Sir Hugo replied, "tea and buns and doubtless eaten in a Vicarage."

As he spoke, he remembered that a Vicarage had been Lorena's home and he thought that he should not have expected her to be anything but a rather parochial young woman, doubtless given to 'good works'.

Then he remembered that, although his brother might have been unworldly. he had been very intelligent and his wife had been the same.

He found it hard to recall very clearly what his sister-in-law had looked like because he had not seen her often.

She had in fact, he was sure, a sweet face and when he went to her funeral everybody he had spoken to had told him how much she would be missed and there had been no doubt of the sincerity in their voices or of the tears in their eyes.

Now he mused Lorena was different in every way from what anyone might have expected even himself.

Aloud he said to her,

"First I must present you to your host, who has been kind enough to invite you to join his party. Alstone, this is my niece. Lorena – the Duke of Windlemere."

Because he looked so magnificent, so imposing and so exactly, Lorena told herself, the way a Duke should look, she bobbed him a little curtsey in the same way that the girls at school had always greeted the Mother Superior.

As his hand took hers, she said,

"Thank you so very much for having me here, Your Grace. It is the marvellous magnificent house that I have dreamt about – but never expected to see."

"I am gratified that Mere should have been in your dreams," the Duke smiled.

"And the next thing she will say is that you are in them too!" came a woman's voice.

It was Daisy Hellingford, who had spoken and Sir Hugo interposed,

"This is my niece, Daisy. She has just returned from Rome, where she has been at school."

He turned to Lorena.

"I don't need to tell you that the Countess of Hellingford is known as being one of the most beautiful women in England."

"That is what Alstone should be saying, not you!" Daisy retorted before Lorena could speak.

There was something fantastic about her green gown, which was extremely décolleté, the huge necklace of emeralds round her neck and the bandeau of the same stones on her head.

Because she was fashionably tall she seemed to tower over Lorena, but, as Sir Hugo drew his niece away to introduce her to the other guests, he thought that she did not seem overawed but merely excited and interested.

To Lorena it seemed as if every man she spoke to was having a secret joke about something with her uncle.

She had no idea what it could be, she only felt rather than heard that it was there in what they said and the way they looked at her.

In some manner that she could not explain it seemed to signify their approval of something he had done, but she did not know what it could be.

When dinner was announced, the Duke proceeded in first with Lady Hellingford on his arm and a man called Lord Carnforth told Lorena that he was to take her in to dinner.

As they walked down the wide passage that led to the dining room, Lorena asked,

"Do you know this house – well?

"Very well," Lord Carnforth replied. "I stay here as frequently as your uncle does."

"And does it seem just as exciting to you now as it did the first time – you ever came here?"

"That was a long time ago. I have almost forgotten my special feelings at that time. I do, of course, still think that it is one of the finest houses in England, which indeed it is."

"That is what I thought you would say," Lorena answered. "And I want to remember exactly what I feel – every moment I am here."

"Why?"

"So that if I never come here again I shall always remember it and I must not miss anything of what to me – is a wonderful and exciting adventure."

CHAPTER THREE

The Duke at dinner had placed the Countess on his left and the Marchioness of Trumpington on his right.

As he wanted to watch Lorena, he had seated her as the next lady beyond the Countess so that he could both see and hear her.

He had been rather surprised at her appearance, because despite her youth she looked distinctive.

Although he noticed the simplicity of her inexpensive dress, like her uncle he realised that it had an individuality that made it completely and absolutely right for her.

He imagined that somebody must have helped her choose it.

Doubtless in Rome there were dressmakers who had a true artistic sense, not like those in London who followed the fashion blindly without taking into consideration the different appearances of their clients.

Looking down the table laden with gold ornaments, the white tablecloth decorated at the sides with wreaths of flowers and in the centre a profusion of purple orchids, the Duke thought that it would be difficult not to notice Lorena.

Her youth and her plain white gown seemed to stand out so that if it had been a stage set she would have been the star on whom the audience's attention was focused while everybody else faded into the background.

It was just a passing thought and he told himself cynically that he must be getting to the age where youth had an attraction of its own.

Then he thought angrily that he was not old enough yet to be looking back into the past and for a few minutes he responded in a gratifying manner to the blandishments of Daisy Hellingford.

Then once again he found his eyes drawn back to Lorena and told himself that it was because he was the Judge in a contention where a great deal of money was involved.

She was listening to Lord Carnforth with what he thought was an almost rapt attention and, as Daisy lowered her voice and said something especially for his ears, he could hear Archie holding forth on the merits of his racehorses.

It was a subject that he was always pleased to discuss in detail and the Duke thought that it was rather clever of Lorena to have started him off on it so early in the evening.

He did not know that Lorena had remembered that once when her mother had been reading out to her father the names of the guests at a very smart party where his brother had been present he had remarked,

"I remember Carnforth as a young boy coming to stay at home. I did not realise then, of course, that he would be so successful as to win the Derby."

"I would love to go to the Derby, Papa," Lorena had exclaimed.

Her father had looked at her in surprise.

"Why?" he asked,

"I saw a reproduction of a fantastic painting by William Frith," she replied, "and it told me that the Derby must be a wonderful sight."

Her father smiled.

"It is. I remember going there when I was at Oxford University and the crowds on the Heath, the gypsies and the coaches remained in my mind long after the race itself."

"That is what to me would be so fascinating," Lorena said, "and I am sure that your friend must have been very proud when he won the most famous race in the world."

"Who told you it was that?" her father asked in an amused voice.

"That was the description I read in *The Times.*"

"One day I hope you will see a Derby," her father said lightly. "But it seems at the moment very unlikely that I shall ever do so again."

This had been a casual conversation, but, when Lord Carnforth escorted her in to dinner, Lorena had recalled and she reminded him of how he had stayed with her grandfather.

"Good Heavens! That was a long time ago," he said. "It was soon after I met your uncle and, as he was in his last year at Oxford and I in my first, I was extremely flattered when he asked me to stay."

"And you have been close friends ever since,"

"I suppose one might say so," Lord Carnforth replied, remembering how often he disagreed with Sir Hugo.

"Did you have a horse running in the Derby this year?" Lorena asked him.

"As a matter of fact I did, but he was unplaced. I had hopes for him, only to be disappointed."

"What happened?" Lorena asked sympathetically.

Immediately Lord Carnforth was off, telling her about his horses, about his special methods of training them and how he was usually right in predicting exactly how they would run and where they would be placed.

If he had been speaking to one of the other ladies they would doubtless have found the subject, which was all too familiar, extremely boring.

But to Lorena it was new and, as she gave Lord Carnforth her full attention, she realised that this was not only the greatest interest he had but was undoubtedly the love of his life.

He paused for a moment and she asked,

"Do you consider that the way you feed your horses is important?"

"Of course it is," Lord Carnforth exclaimed. "I have gone to a great deal of trouble to study the different ways of feeding racehorses and I have worked out a method of my own that usually proves extremely successful."

He paused as if for effect and Lorena went on,

"This may sound a strange question, but are you equally particular about the water they drink?"

Lord Carnforth looked at her and then raised his eyebrows in surprise.

"I am asking you this," Lorena continued, "because in Rome, when if it rains excessively, the Tiber floods and there have been reports of a great deal of illness in the lower parts of the City."

She looked at Lord Carnforth to see if he was listening and then carried on,

"Although there is anxiety about the effect of bad water- on human beings, no one ever seems to worry about the animals, which surely can be upset too."

Lord Carnforth looked at her for a moment and then said,

"That is a very interesting theory, which I must say had never struck me. I always take my horses' food anywhere they are racing, but I have never thought of taking the water that they are accustomed to drinking."

The Duke, who had been listening to the last part of the conversation and ignoring something particularly provocative that the Countess was saying to him, bent forward to remark,

"It never struck me, Archie, that water could be important in the training of horses, but now that I think of it, it appears to be sheer common sense and, what is more, I suspect that the water in some of the stables in which we put our horses before a race is definitely unclean."

"Water varies all over the country – " Lord Carnforth began and then he exclaimed,

"Do you know, I believe this child is right! I now remember at a Race Meeting three weeks ago noticing that my horses seemed to dislike the water that they were being given and the buckets too were dirty."

"It certainly gives us a new explanation," the Duke said, "as to why horses which seem perfectly fit when they leave home fail in a race when they should, by all statistics, win easily."

Because the Duke was speaking, the men at his end of the table were all listening and now an argument began, which in a very short time involved the whole table.

There was not a man amongst the Duke's friends who, if he was not an actual racehorse owner, was not deeply interested in the 'Sport of Kings'.

Now they were all expressing their opinions on what to them was an entirely new idea,

It was quite a long time and several courses later when the gentleman on Lorena's other side said with a smile,

"You certainly seem to have started something. Who suggested to you in the first place that what they drink might affect the running of horses?"

"When I spoke of water to Lord Carnforth," Lorena replied, "I was actually thinking that, if it is polluted or dirty, it must affect all animals and, of course, in Rome the Nuns always warned us to be careful of what we drank when we went into the City."

"I gather then that your school was outside."

Lorena nodded.

"It was in a very beautiful position with a fine view especially of St. Peter's."

"I have not been to Rome for a long time," her partner said, "but I remember being very impressed with the Coliseum and, of course, the many fountains."

"They are beautiful," Lorena agreed. "I am so lucky to have been educated in a place that makes one want instinctively to learn and which is so redolent of history."

"I hope you are interested in the present as well as the past," the man beside her remarked and there was something slightly flirtatious in his voice.

"But naturally" Lorena replied. "And in the future."

As she spoke, she remembered that she had no idea what her future might hold.

Just for a moment she looked anxious and glanced at her uncle, who was farther down the table, hoping that he would think that she was behaving in the right way and perhaps would not be in too much of a hurry to be rid of her.

"What is worrying you?"

The man on her right was a Major in what had been her uncle's Regiment, the Life Guards, and his name was Kelvin Fane. Although Lorena was not aware of it, he was heir presumptive to a Dukedom.

He was one of the most sought after men in London and, although he had an extremely able brain and would have done well in Politics, he preferred to stay in his Regiment.

Because it was always stationed in London he spent his time flirting with beautiful women, 'moving relentlessly,' as one wag put it, 'from *boudoir to boudoir*!'

He had never looked at a young and marriageable girl and his only interest in Lorena now was that he had a bet and quite a considerable one that Hugo Benson was bound to lose to Lord Carnforth.

Now, watching Lorena, he was not so sure.

He liked the way she spoke, her soft musical voice, her unselfconsciousness and the way that she looked straight into the eyes of the person she was talking to.

She was smiling as she spoke to him now and he thought that in a few years' time she would be the sort of beauty who would turn men's heads and it would be a pity if by that time he was too old to pursue her.

While the rest of the guests at the table were still talking about racehorses and water, impulsively and without really considering if he should do so, Major Fane dropped his voice to say,

"And what do you expect to find in the future, love or marriage?"

"Surely they are synonymous," Lorena replied. "And I suppose that is what I would – like to find – eventually."

"Why not at once?"

"Because, while it may sound rather foolish to you, there are so many places in the world I would like to visit and so much I want to learn."

She saw that he looked surprised and she explained,

"I have, been at school for the last three years. Rome is beautiful, but the world is very big."

Major Fane laughed at the way she spoke.

"Very big," he agreed. "But you cannot expect to go exploring by yourself and, if you were married, your husband would doubtless take you to Paris. All pretty women want to go to Paris."

"Why?" Lorena enquired.

"Because it is the City of gaiety and love and the French know how to accommodate lovers better than any other nation in the world."

"You mean – they specialise in it?" Lorena asked. "How strange."

"Why strange?"

"Because surely everybody, regardless of where they are born, wants to love and – be loved. I cannot think why the French should think it is exclusive to their nation."

Major Fane smiled.

"That is a question that you will know the answer to when you are older."

"Perhaps no one will want to – take me to Paris."

The Major laughed.

"I can reassure you by telling you that a great number of men will suggest that very thing, of course, after the Wedding ring is on your finger."

There was a touch of cynicism in his voice and Lorena looked puzzled for a moment before she said,

"Before I go to Paris, there is a great deal in England I want to see, besides other parts of the world."

She gave a little sigh and then went on,

"But I expect most of it will have to remain where it is already – in a book or in my mind. I have no money to travel with."

"That again can easily be remedied, if you choose a rich husband."

Lorena laughed.

"I arrived back in England from school today and I think I may have to wait for a long time before anybody asks me to be his wife. Besides – I should want to be very much in love before I accepted."

Major Fane raised his eyebrows.

"Has Kitty heard you talk like this?" he asked.

"No, I have not seen my aunt for three years."

"Then I warn you, if Kitty arranges your marriage, she will not consider the dictates of your heart, only the size of the applicant's Bank balance!"

Major Fane was speaking in a manner that would have made the women who he usually associated with scream with laughter and declare him to be wickedly witty.

But Lorena merely looked worried.

"You are – frightening me," she murmured after a moment. "Although I am sure it is unnecessary, because I decided a long time ago that I would never marry anyone unless I was in love with him."

Major Fane was just about to tell her that her ideas were not only out of date but extremely impracticable in the social life enjoyed by her uncle and aunt.

Then somehow he changed the words he was about to say and, in a very different voice from the one he had used before, he said quietly,

"Then I hope, Miss Benson, you will fall in love with somebody who loves you and, of course, you both live happily ever after."

He was not being cynical and he spoke with a sincerity that surprised himself.

Instantly the smile was back on Lorena's lips and in her eyes.

"Thank you," she said, "that is just what I would like to hear, especially tonight when I am here."

Major Fane wondered what she meant by that, but before he could ask her for an explanation, the lady on his other side attracted his attention and Lorena turned back to Lord Carnforth.

"Now look what you have done with your revolutionary ideas!" he exclaimed. "You have got everybody arguing. I don't mind telling you that either the Duke or I will bring up this whole subject at the next Jockey Club meeting."

"I do hope I shall be able to hear the result," Lorena said.

"I promise I will tell you what they say," Lord Carnforth replied.

"Thank you. I should like to think of your horses winning every race you enter them for simply because they were given the right sort of water."

When the ladies had left the room, Lord Carnforth moved up to sit next to the Duke and Sir Hugo came from the other end of the table to sit near them.

"What started that extraordinary argument about water of all things?" he asked, "It is not a liquid I usually associate with a dinner party at Mere!"

The Duke laughed.

"I should hope not! But it was in fact your niece's idea in the first place."

"Lorena's?" Sir Hugo asked in astonishment. "I do not believe it!"

"It's true," Archie Carnforth said. "I have to admit, Hugo, that she has an original mind if nothing else."

"I cannot remember when we last had a discussion at dinner that involved every man present," the Duke observed.

There was a twist to his lips as he added, "Daisy informed me that it was the most boring meal that she had ever spent in my company."

Sir Hugo looked at him apprehensively.

"For Heaven's sake," he said in a low voice, "don't let Daisy get her knife into Lorena. She dislikes women anyway and a child straight from school is hardly up to her weight."

"No, indeed," the Duke nodded.

"Nevertheless it is an extremely interesting idea," Lord Carnforth was saying. "In point of fact I am now certain that it was what was wrong with my horse – "

He was off again on the subject of his horses and the rest of the men who had intended to say something about Lorena found themselves side-tracked into the same argument until the Duke signalled that it was time to join the ladies.

Both he and Sir Hugo entered the drawing room wondering what they would find.

They were well aware that it was a much more demanding test for Lorena to be with the women than with the men.

Sir Hugo half-suspected that he would find his niece sitting outside the group and feeling rather shy and possibly tongue-tied.

To his surprise and to the Duke's she was deep in conversation with, of all people, the Marchioness of Trumpington.

Enid Trumpington had been a beauty who had married a man far older than herself, one who had given her a social position that she would not have been entitled to as a young girl.

Beautiful with red hair and skin that was the envy of her contemporaries she was extremely passionate. Her love affairs, which followed one another in quick succession, had given the Social world something to talk about for the last ten years.

She was at the moment being extremely indiscreet with Lord Gilmour, who was also a guest at Mere.

Lord Gilmour had the misfortune of being married to a woman who was always ill, always complaining and preferred to live in the country.

Everybody had been extremely sorry for him as he was a man who enjoyed gaiety, good living and the company of beautiful women and, when he first started his *affaire de coeur* with Enid Trumpington, it had been considered quite suitable.

Now they were, as Daisy Hellingford herself had said tartly, 'making an exhibition of themselves'.

It seemed to everybody that it was only a question of time before both the Marquis and Lady Gilmour became aware of what was happening.

The Marquis of Trumpington was getting old, but he was important in Court circles and because of his long experience he was still greatly in demand by the new King.

The fact that he was so often in attendance at Buckingham Palace or Windsor Castle left the Marchioness with a great deal of freedom that she would otherwise not have had and she and Lord Gilmour made the most of it.

They were, however, overstepping the bounds of behaviour that had been summed up during the last reign in one very pertinent command,

"Thou shalt not cause a scandal!"

There were whispers that Jack Gilmour and Enid Trumpington had been seen alone together in Paris.

And it was all too painfully obvious when they were at parties that they had eyes for no one but each other.

The Duke, who had had a flirtation with Enid some years earlier, was well aware that her fiery and insatiable nature made it difficult for her to be restrained or discreet

Yet he thought that Gilmour would have had more sense and he decided that during this week at Mere he would speak to him and suggest, as a good friend, that he should observe the proprieties more closely.

Things had changed in the last three years and under the new King and Queen the codes of behaviour had become very much more conventional.

King George V and Queen Mary were propriety itself and, although in consequence the Court was much duller and, the Duke thought, very boring, there was no doubt that they were setting new standards that, unless they would invite disaster, must be followed by all those who wished to be accepted in the best Society.

He wondered, as he walked down the length of the long and beautiful room, what Enid Trumpington could possibly have to say to a girl as young as Lorena.

He only hoped that she was not being unpleasant to the child as he and Hugo were afraid that Daisy might be.

He would have liked to go up to the Marchioness and find out what she was discussing with Lorena.

Instead, as if in duty bound, he moved to Daisy Hellingford's side.

"Alstone, are we going to play bridge?" she enquired. "Or perhaps a game of baccarat would be fun. I am sick to death of horses! I never want to hear of one again."

"We will do whatever you like," the Duke said good-humouredly. "It shall be baccarat, if you prefer."

As he spoke, he knew that this meant that he would pay any losses that Daisy incurred, while she would keep her winnings.

But if she was amused he was quite prepared to concur.

"It shall be baccarat," Daisy decided.

She clapped her hands and called out in a loud voice,

"Who is prepared to lose a pile of money because tonight I feel my luck is in?"

There was some laughter and some slightly sarcastic remarks at this, but those who wished to play moved across the drawing room and into the anteroom, where gaming tables of every sort were ready for anyone who felt inclined to use them.

As the Duke had not dared to do, Sir Hugo walked up to the Marchioness of Trumpington to say,

"I can see that you are being very kind, Enid, to my niece. I am grateful because I am sure that you are aware it must be quite an ordeal to arrive here as she has, knowing only one person, and that her uncle."

"A very attractive uncle, which, of course, makes a difference," the Marchioness replied, who could never resist flattering any man whether she was interested in him or not.

"Thank you, Enid. May I say how lovely you look tonight, although it's not surprising."

The Marchioness smiled and rose to her feet.

"I must go and play with Jack," she said, "otherwise he will lose to Daisy every penny he possesses, which is something I have no intention of allowing."

She paused for a moment before she moved away to say to Lorena,

"You and I, dear, must have another talk again soon."

Lorena had stood up politely when the Marchioness rose and now Sir Hugo sat down in the chair she had vacated and asked,

"What were you talking about?"

"She was telling me how she felt and what she did when she was my age."

Sir Hugo looked surprised, but before he could ask her more, Major Fane came towards them and said,

"I am sure that there is something quite wrong in an uncle and niece sitting together. It is almost as bad as one of those official dinners where a man has always to sit beside his wife."

"If by that you mean to talk to Lorena," Sir Hugo said, "I am delighted to concede that you have a prior claim, as you did not sit next to her at dinner."

"I was going to suggest," Major Fane said, "that she might like to watch the gambling. What takes place at Mere is quite an education in itself."

"It is very kind of you," Lorena answered, "and it is something I would – like to do. But first, would it be very rude if I – looked at the paintings – in this room?"

She spoke a little hesitatingly and glanced at Sir Hugo as if she feared that he might think it incorrect.

But her uncle merely smiled,

"It is rather clever of you as it happens," he said, "for Major Fane will inherit one of the finest collections of paintings in the country and there is no one who knows more about them than him."

As Lorena rose eagerly from the chair she was sitting in, he added,

"He is a walking guidebook so make the most of it while you have the opportunity."

"I shall," Lorena replied so fervently that both her uncle and Major Fane laughed.

*

Lorena awoke and thought with delight that it was morning.

She told herself last night when she went to bed very late by Convent standards that she begrudged every moment that she must waste in sleeping when there were so many fascinating and exciting things to see and do at Mere.

"There are no plans for tomorrow," the Duke had said before they went up to bed, "and most of you have been here often enough to know that everything I own is at your disposal and you have only to ask for anything you want."

Because there were expressions of surprise on the faces of some of his guests, he explained,

"I am saying this because there is somebody here who has never stayed at Mere before, but doubtless her uncle had told her what to expect."

"I have hardly had time," Sir Hugo protested, "so you tell her, Alstone. It comes much better from you."

"Very well," the Duke concurred and then turned to Lorena to say,

"As everybody else knows, there is tennis, croquet, golf, horses to ride if you prefer and punts on the lake, although I beg you not to trust yourself to Fane, who got stuck in the mud last time he attempted to squire a lovely lady."

"That was *his* story!" somebody piped up, laughing. "And Miss Benson is too young to be allowed in a punt alone with Kelvin."

There was more laughter and the Duke thought that Lorena looked a little shy and he went on,

"There are not only horses in the stables to ride but you can be driven anywhere you wish or, if you prefer, there are cars at your disposal. I suppose that there are other amusements, but I cannot think of them at the moment."

"Kelvin will fill in the gaps very eloquently," one man teased.

Lorena wondered why there were so many jokes about Major Fane.

He had been so kind in showing her the paintings not only in the drawing room but also in several of the other rooms as well.

There had been some remarks that she had not understood when they had returned to the Blue Drawing Room and she had thought that the Viscountess Storr had spoken to the Major in rather a sharp manner.

Lorena had not noticed her before, but she was a tall, dark attractive woman with a deep slow voice that reminded Lorena of a purring cat.

She had looked across at the Major when they reappeared and said,

"I never imagined cradle snatching was particularly in your line, Kelvin!"

"But paintings are, Sarah," he answered, "and Sir Hugo asked me to show them to his niece."

The Viscountess had shrugged her shoulders and walked away in a manner that Lorena knew showed that she was angry.

Because she thought that it must have been her fault for keeping the Major so long out of the drawing room, she was just about to apologise when the Duke joined them.

"You enjoyed seeing my paintings?" he asked Lorena.

"You have a very beautiful collection, Your Grace, far better than anything I have seen in Rome. But then I have always preferred the English artists and your Constables are magnificent."

The Duke looked at her in surprise and Major Fane with a twinkle in his eyes pointed out,

"You will find that Miss Benson knows a great deal about paintings."

He moved away as he spoke and Lorena remarked,

"I wanted to – thank him."

"You will have plenty of time to do so," the Duke said. "Now tell me which of my paintings that you have seen so far is your favourite?"

He thought that like most people who visited Mere she would find it almost impossible to pick out anything in particular, but instead she answered him without any hesitation,

"The Romneys, but that is not only because of the artist but the subject."

"You mean those he painted of Emma Hamilton?" the Duke enquired.

"Yes."

"You admire the redoubtable Lady Hamilton?"

"I admire her because she not only educated and improved herself – until she could entertain the most important people in Naples, including the King and Queen," Lorena answered, "but she also inspired – the greatest sailor England has ever known."

She spoke with such enthusiasm that the Duke was amused.

"Are you really condoning an illicit love affair?" he asked. "Surely you remember that Lady Hamilton had a husband and Lord Nelson had a wife?"

There was a pause for a moment and he saw the colour rise faintly in Lorena's cheeks.

"I had not really – thought of it – like that," she said. "I was remembering how she persuaded the King of Naples to allow the British Fleet to shelter in their Ports when at first the Napolese had refused because they were frightened of Napoleon."

She paused for a moment before she added,

"If they had not been able to do that, there would never have been the Battle of the Nile when Napoleon's Fleet was completely annihilated."

"I am recalling my history now," the Duke smiled, "but I am still interested that a woman who was in love with a man who was not her husband should command your admiration."

"I think perhaps – that part of the story was rather glossed over in our history books," Lorena said a little hesitatingly, "but helping and inspiring Lord Nelson could not be – wrong. And if it was activated by love, then we must forgive her, considering how much she did for England."

The Duke was rather intrigued.

He had somehow expected that a girl coming from a Convent, and certainly one so young, would have been shocked and even horrified by anything that concerned an illicit liaison.

But from what Lorena had said he was quite certain that she did not understand the full story of Emma Hamilton's wild infatuation for Lord Nelson and his for her.

But she was certainly not condemning, as he had thought she would, a married woman who had loved another man.

He wondered what Lorena would say if she knew of the intrigues and affairs that were taking place at Mere at this particular moment.

There was not one man in the party, with the exception of Sir Hugo, who was not involved with one of the women present.

Hugo Benson was, to the Duke's knowledge, captivated by an extremely attractive lady. But he had deliberately not invited her to Mere. To make the numbers right, Hugo had to partner Lorena.

Also the Duke was certain, from all he knew of young girls, which was very little, that Lorena would be shocked if she had any idea that there was anything irregular in her uncle and aunt's relationship.

The whole of the Windlemere Set was aware that Hugo and Kitty had not been getting on, both having had separate interests for some years, but as that was nothing unusual and applied to almost every other married couple, it had long ago ceased to be a subject of any interest.

Now the Duke said,

"I hope tomorrow, or at least while you are staying here, you will look at my Romneys with me. I shall be interested to hear more of your comments on the beautiful Emma."

Lorena appeared to be thinking for a moment and then she responded,

"There is so much I want to see and – so much I would like to know and learn about the treasures you have here, Your Grace. Surely you have a Curator who would not mind answering my questions?"

"I have one, but I am perfectly prepared to answer your questions myself."

"I am sure that you would find all I want to know tedious, even if you had the time," Lorena insisted.

She was not speaking flirtatiously as any other woman might have done, waiting for the Duke to assure her that he would always have the time where she was concerned. She was just stating a fact and she was obviously anxious not to be a nuisance.

"I am perfectly willing to be a most informative guide," the Duke said, "but in case I am not available you will find my Curator, Mr. Gordon Ashley, very knowledgeable and any of the servants will take you to his office."

"Thank you very much, Your Grace."

"Do you intend to spend all tomorrow sightseeing?"

"Not all day" Lorena replied. "You did say that your guests could ride. Since Uncle Hugo was kind enough to pay for the lessons, I have been riding in Rome, but the horses there were very docile."

"I can assure you that mine are quite the opposite," the Duke declared.

"That is what I was hoping," Lorena smiled.

She remembered the conversation now and decided that early in the morning would be a good time to go riding before anybody was about.

She jumped out of bed and went to the window to pull back the curtains.

It was very early and the mist that still lay over the lake swirled round the trunks of the trees on the other side of it.

The sun, however, was rapidly dispersing it and giving the garden and everything she could see a kind of golden glow.

Lorena made a little sound of sheer delight and began to dress herself. .

She had a riding habit which, although it was not very smart, had been made in England and was therefore well cut.

She struggled into it thinking that, although it was shabby because she had had it before she went to Italy, it was unlikely that anyone would see her and therefore it would not really matter.

She glanced at the clock on the mantelpiece and saw that it was only five-thirty and, being sure that she could ride unseen, she decided not to wear a hat.

She arranged her hair simply and with plenty of hairpins so that it should not become untidy, took a last quick glance at herself in the mirror and opened her bedroom door and walked very quietly down the stairs.

As she expected, the front door was open and the steps were being scrubbed by two housemaids in mobcaps.

There were also a number of footmen without their powdered wigs and liveried coats hurrying about in their shirtsleeves and crested-buttoned waistcoats.

They looked at Lorena in surprise, but she merely said, 'good morning' and hurried out through the front door to turn towards the stables.

She knew where they were for her uncle had pointed them out yesterday afternoon as they had driven down the oak-bordered drive that led up to the great house.

"The stables are older than the Robert Adam building," he had told her, "and they are believed to be the finest in the country, but I suspect that you will be more interested in what they contain."

Lorena thought now that she was interested in both and was only hoping that she was not so early that the grooms would still be asleep.

But, as she went through the arch that led to the stables, she saw the horses with their heads over the open half-doors of their stalls and a number of stable lads carrying water buckets and bales of hay.

She stopped the first one she came to.

"Good morning. His Grace has said that I could ride. I wonder if somebody could saddle me a horse."

"Yes, of course, ma'am," the stable boy answered.

He put down his bucket and went through an open door and Lorena followed him.

She found that in this part of the stables the stalls did not look out onto the yard and, as she walked down the passage, she looked at the horses thinking each one finer than the last.

"Good mornin'," came a respectful voice beside her and she looked round to find an elderly groom.

"I understands you wish to ride, ma'am."

"Yes, please," Lorena answered him eagerly.

"One nice and quiet, mebbe?

"Not *too* quiet."

"I got just the right mount for a lady," the groom said smiling. "This one 'ere."

He stepped into one of the stalls and, as he did so, Lorena saw a large stallion in the next stall, which a groom was saddling.

As if without asking the question the groom was aware of her curiosity, he said,

"That be for 'Is Grace, ma'am. I expects as you're up ever so early, you'll be a-ridin' with 'im."

"I had no idea that he would be riding so early," Lorena answered, "but I would like to do so, if he would not feel it an intrusion."

"Not 'im ma'am!" the groom replied. "The truth be that 'Is Grace is so energetic 'e's up afore anyone else in the 'ouse 'as their eyes open."

He gave a chuckle as he added,

"It'll be a surprise to 'Is Grace to see you 'ere so bright and early."

He was right, Lorena thought, as a few minutes later she followed the groom as he led the horse round to the front door for the Duke.

The Duke was already there waiting and she noticed looking extremely smart in his breeches and highly polished boots and wearing a whipcord riding jacket that had obviously been cut by a Master hand.

His tall hat was on the side of his dark head and he carried a crop.

There was no mistaking his astonishment as he saw Lorena.

"You are up very early, Miss Benson!" he exclaimed.

"I thought I would be the only person who would wish to ride before breakfast," Lorena answered, "But if you would rather be alone, I can easily ride by myself."

"I would not be so ungallant as to suggest such an idea. We will ride together and I only hope, after all you have said, that my horse is spirited enough for you."

"I shall be very embarrassed if he is too spirited and throws me off or I cannot control him," Lorena replied with a smile.

The Duke mounted the stallion that was being held for him.

"That is something we shall have to prove," he said and they set off side by side.

Then, as they crossed the bridge that spanned the lake, the Duke asked almost automatically,

"Are you all right?"

"I was just thinking, Your Grace, that I definitely am dreaming. I am riding a magnificent horse and I am staying in the most majestic house I have ever seen. I do hope I shall not wake up – too quickly,"

The Duke laughed.

"I hope so too. But surely there is someone in your dream you have omitted to mention?"

For a moment Lorena did not understand and then she smiled.

"If you mean you," she said, "of course you are magnificent too! Mr. Gillingham said that you are Prince Charming, and I am sure you are aware that this is exactly who you are."

She spoke naturally without any touch of self-consciousness and, the Duke thought wryly, he was not certain if it was a compliment at all.

Then he was aware that Lorena was no longer thinking of him but concentrating on her riding and, he sensed, longing to gallop as soon as they were clear of the trees,

'She is certainly unpredictable,' he told himself and settled down to follow her as she forged ahead.

CHAPTER FOUR

Driving to Church the Duke found himself thinking about Lorena.

It was only a short distance and it was a tradition that in the winter he drove in his closed brougham and in the summer in an open Victoria, as his father and mother had always done.

If he had suggested going by car, he was quite certain that there would have been a revolution amongst the old servants.

When Robert Adam had built Mere on the site of an older house, he had not, as was usual for the period, included a private Chapel because there was already a very beautiful Norman Church just inside the park.

It was part of the history of the family and the elaborate tombs, added to down the centuries, enriched the ancient building.

It was the Duke's father who had decided that the whole household must attend Church on Sundays and that the Service should be at seven-thirty in the morning, which would entail less inconvenience than if it was held at a later hour.

Accordingly a long line of servants walked the quarter-of-a-mile down the drive to the Church, headed by the butler and Mrs. Kingston and followed by the other servants in order of seniority down to the youngest and most newly joined knife-boy.

The Duke habitually arrived at two minutes to the half hour and he would have been extremely annoyed if, owing to any oversight by his valet or lack of punctuality on the part of his coachman, he was even a few seconds late.

It was when the Victoria crossed over the bridge that he found himself regretting that this morning he would miss his ride and be unable to accompany Lorena as he had done yesterday.

He was quite certain that she would take the opportunity of riding one of his horses again.

It had given her such pleasure that when they had finished their first gallop he had seen that her eyes were shining like stars and her whole face seemed to have lit up as a child's might have done at some unexpected treat,

Yesterday they had ridden for very nearly an hour before the Duke said,

"It is now nearly half-past-six. Are you feeling hungry?"

"Now that you mention it, I am," Lorena replied. "I was too excited to eat very much dinner last night, delicious though it was."

"Then I think you are entitled to a good breakfast. Follow me."

He rode on ahead before she could reply and a few minutes later she saw in front of her an old and very attractive farmhouse.

It had stood on the estate for many centuries and was built of red brick and ships' timbers and its gabled roof and twisted chimneys were a complement to its diamond-paned casements.

Despite its most picturesque appearance, it was, however, a farmhouse with cocks and hens pecking pieces of grain in a yard at the side of it, a number of cows with their calves in a field at the back and on the pond, which was bordered by yellow kingcups, were dozens of fat white ducks.

"It is the prettiest farm I have ever seen!" Lorena exclaimed.

After a farm lad had taken their horses from them, they had walked into a large flagged kitchen with hams hung from the low beams and the farmer's wife came hurrying to greet them as she wiped her hands on her apron.

"Good mornin', Your Grace," she said to the Duke, dropping a curtsey. "It's real nice to see you! When I 'eard you were up at the Big 'Ouse I was 'opin' you'd call in on us."

"I am not only feeling hungry for one of your excellent breakfasts, Mrs. Swallow," the Duke replied, "but I have brought a guest who I know will find your eggs and ham as delicious as I do."

"You be very welcome 'ere," Mrs. Swallow said to Lorena.

She led the way across the kitchen and into what she called 'the parlour'.

It was a somewhat stiff room with an upright piano, framed texts embroidered in wool on the walls and a bow-fronted window that had a good view over the undulating green meadows to the distant hills, which made Lorena exclaim with delight.

"I always say that Hundle Farm has a better view than I have at Mere," the Duke remarked.

"It's lovely!" Lorena cried. "But so far I have found nothing amongst your possessions that is anything else."

"That is just what I like to hear," the Duke said complacently.

He sat down at the round table that was set in the window and, when Mrs. Swallow had covered it with a white cloth, she brought in everything that Lorena associated with a farm.

A cottage loaf, hot and crisp from the oven, a huge pat of golden butter, a comb of honey that came from the hives she could see in the field outside and a few minutes later a large plate of eggs with slices of ham.

"It be fortunate, Your Grace, that we 'ave an 'am just ready to eat," Mrs. Swallow smiled.

"I am hoping I may have another of your hams up at the house," the Duke asked her. "There is no one in the whole district, as you well know, Mrs. Swallow, who can cure a ham as well as you."

"'Tis a secret as 'as bin 'anded down from me great-grandmother," Mrs. Swallow replied. "And it be nice to know Your Grace appreciates it."

"I do indeed," the Duke answered.

Anticipating what he might require when he had finished the eggs, Mrs. Swallow brought in a newly carved cold ham, which, when Lorena had eaten a few slices, she thought was more delicious than any ham she had ever tasted before.

"I am afraid I am being rather – greedy."

"I am glad you are young enough to enjoy simple things like a farm breakfast," the Duke commented.

"It's delicious! Do you always come here when you go riding?"

"When I am alone."

"But you brought me."

"As I have said, I thought you would enjoy a farm breakfast, while most of the ladies who stay at Mere only toy with a cup of coffee."

"I hope I shall never get like that."

"Are you anticipating that you might?" the Duke asked.

"I am afraid that Uncle Hugo and Aunt Kitty, if I stay with them, will want me to behave in a fashionable manner – but actually I think they will send me – away, to live with one of my – other relations."

There was no doubt that the idea was worrying her and the Duke said after a moment,

"Your aunt is very fond of London. Is that what you would enjoy?"

"I think it would be unfair if I said 'no' because I have never been to parties, but what I would really like would be to live in the country with horses to ride – and perhaps have a few real friends – not a whole crowd of – acquaintances."

Lorena spoke slowly and seriously, as if she was thinking out what she was saying and then, before the Duke could reply, she said,

"I think farmers are very lucky because they must feel like God."

"Like God?" the Duke repeated. "What do you mean by that?"

Lorena gave him a little smile that was almost apologetic.

"It came into my mind when I saw the calves and the lambs and the chickens and the piglets that farmers are always creating new life. Every year young animals are born and that in itself must not only be exciting but must give them a feeling of omnipotence."

The Duke laughed.

"I have never heard that idea before. You certainly seem to be full of originality."

Lorena glanced at him quickly as if she thought that she might have said something wrong and, without her having to ask the question, the Duke observed,

"Originality is what most people lack. I am just wondering where those ideas of yours come from."

"Out of my head," Lorena replied disarmingly.

"And who have you discussed them with before?"

"Not many people. The girls at school wanted to talk about the things they had done in the holidays and, as I never came home, I could not join in with them in that. Otherwise they talked about what they were going to do when they left school and I had no idea what would happen to me."

"Are you telling me that you talk to yourself?" the Duke quizzed her.

"Not really." Lorena smiled. "I think to myself and make up stories, but I never dreamt that I would ever see a house as magnificent as yours and have the opportunity to admire the treasures it contains. Yours at Mere are fantastic!"

"You have not yet seen all of them,"

"Perhaps – there will not be – time to see the rest."

She gave a little sigh and added,

"'I do hope Uncle Hugo will not want to – leave until I have – seen everything."

"Let me reassure you by saying that, as far as I know, your uncle is quite prepared to stay for nearly a week."

"That is what I hoped and thank you, thank you, thank you very much, Your Grace, for having me here."

"If I say it's a pleasure," the Duke replied, "that will sound rather trite as the polite remark one always makes, but actually on this occasion it is the truth."

She gave him a smile as if he had given her a very special present and then helped herself to another slice of ham.

'She is completely natural,' the Duke thought now as the carriage proceeded down the drive towards the Church.

He recalled how, as they rode home when Mere came into sight, Lorena had said,

"I suppose we – have to go – back? I would like to go on riding for – hours and hours and – miles and miles."

"There are other days for you to ride."

"Yes, I know, but I wish just the same – that sometimes that time – could stand – still."

There was something in her voice that made him ask,

"I wonder if you are telling me in a rather roundabout way that you have been a little apprehensive or shy of meeting all the people who are staying with me?"

It would have been, he thought as he spoke, understandable for any young girl to feel like that and it was what they had all expected of Lorena before she had arrived.

And yet she had not behaved at all in the way that Archie Carnforth had said she would.

She answered,

"Mama always used to say that being shy was a form of selfishness as one was thinking about oneself instead of other people."

"But surely," the Duke insisted, "you were just a little shy when you first arrived here?"

"There did seem to be a number of – butterflies fluttering – inside me," Lorena confessed, "but, when I saw – you, I forgot about – myself."

"Why me?" the Duke enquired.

"Because you are exactly what I had hoped the owner of my dream house would look like and Mr. Gillingham had said Mere is 'like a Fairy Palace'."

"I am glad I did not disappoint you."

"No, you were just right and so was everybody else – the beautiful ladies glittering with jewels and moving as gracefully as swans in their evening gowns, the flowers on the table at dinner, the paintings, the gold ornaments – I shall always remember it."

Now thinking over what she had said, the Duke thought to himself that she was seeing everything as if it was a painting and perceptively he guessed that neither he nor the rest of the party was to her really human.

Lorena was a child watching a play upon a stage, entranced and absorbed in what she saw and heard, but not feeling that it was in any way personal or that she was actually part of it.

He did not know why he understood that he only felt as if in some way he could read her thoughts and sense the feeling that she had tried to put into words.

With a little start he realised that the carriage had reached the Church,

He could see the Vicar in his white surplice waiting in the porch to receive him and escort him up the aisle to the huge carved family pew that was situated in the Chancel.

He stepped out of the carriage and held out his hand,

"Good morning, Vicar."

"Good morning, Your Grace. It is a great honour to have you worship with us once again."

These formal words were always spoken on such occasions and, without waiting for the Duke's reply, the Vicar went ahead and they were led by the Verger up the aisle between the pews, which were packed with the servants from Mere and a few of the villagers.

Because he had been thinking of Lorena, the Duke was not really surprised to find her already in the family pew.

As the Vicar showed him into the special seat carved with his Coat of Arms and he sat down on the red velvet cushions, he saw that Lorena, with her head tipped upwards, was looking at the beautiful stained-glass window high above the altar.

She was wearing a thin muslin gown for, although it was early in the morning, it was already quite hot.

On her head was the turned-back hat that she had travelled in that gave her a very young appearance and looked somewhat like a halo.

She did not look at the Duke and, wondering if she was really aware of his presence, he thought again how unpredictable she was.

He could not imagine being alone, even in a Church, with any other woman and not find her flashing meaningful glances of intimacy at him and managing even in such a sanctified place to make him aware not only of her femininity but also her interest in him personally.

The Service began and the organ, which had been a present to the Church from the Duke's mother, was played surprisingly well by a resident of the village.

The choir consisted mainly of schoolchildren who were forced to attend and they sang the psalms and the hymns more musically than one would have expected in a small village Church.

Once again it had been the Duke's mother, who had been musical, who had taken a great deal of trouble to see that the choir was well trained and that the choirmaster was paid for his services.

As Lorena had been at a Catholic Convent, the Duke wondered if she would have difficulty finding her way through the English Prayer Book. But, as she appeared to be very at home with it, he decided that she had doubtless attended the British Embassy Church in Rome.

He could hear her joining in the psalms and hymns in a clear young voice that he was sure would have delighted his mother.

The Service was short, which again was traditional, for the last Duke had insisted that no sermon should last more than ten minutes.

If it went on any longer, he would look at his watch and walk out.

The Vicar was therefore careful to keep within the time limit and the Duke was aware that Lorena listened all the time he was speaking and did not fidget.

If there was one thing the Duke disliked, it was a woman who fidgeted all the time and he found Daisy Hellingford's habit of playing with her pearls and twiddling her rings round her fingers increasingly irritating.

"Do you not realise," he had asked her once, "that when you are always moving unnecessarily, you dissipate your energy? I was reading an article by a doctor on that subject only the other day."

"I have all the energy left that you need, dearest Alstone," Daisy had replied, "and sometimes a surplus that is wasted."

There was no mistaking what she was insinuating and the Duke did not criticise her fidgeting again. But he knew that it had begun to annoy him more and more.

The collection plate was handed round and the Duke noticed that Lorena placed a shilling in it.

The Vicar accepted the collection at the altar and then blessed the congregation.

Having knelt for a short time, he then proceeded once again to the Duke's pew, because His Grace always left the Church before the rest of the congregation.

For the first time the Duke leant towards Lorena and spoke to her.

"Will you come back with me?" he asked her.

He knew that the way she obeyed was part of her school training and they walked down the aisle side by side behind the Vicar.

"Goodbye, Your Grace," the Vicar bowed at the door. "It has been an honour and a pleasure to have you with us."

"It was a very interesting sermon, Vicar," the Duke replied. "I must congratulate you."

Actually he had not listened to it, but the elderly man flushed with pleasure.

The carriage was waiting outside, a footman holding open the door.

Lorena looked up at the Duke.

"I walked here," she said.

"I hope you will drive back with me," he replied.

"May I? I would like to."

With a gesture of his hand he indicated that she should step into the carriage first and, as they drove away, he said,

"I suppose I should have anticipated that you might wish to go to Church. How did you know about the Service?"

"I asked Emily, the maid who is looking after me," Lorena replied. "Do none of your other guests go with you to Church on Sunday?"

"I expect most of them attend Services in their own villages when they are at home, as I do," the Duke said evasively. "But, as your father was a Parson, I suppose that as far as you are concerned it is a habit that you are not likely to break."

"I have never wanted to," Lorena replied. "When I am in Church I not only feel near to Papa, but also, as he always said, it gives me the Power to face any difficulties and problems that might arise in the week ahead."

"Power?" the Duke questioned. "What do you mean by that?"

"Papa said that we could draw on a life force that is God Himself. It flows into us when we pray, then if you want to help other people, they can draw on it because it is there inside one."

Lorena spoke quite simply and unaffectedly and the Duke thought over what she had just said before he remarked,

"I think that is an excellent explanation of what religion should do for people, but too often it fails lamentably."

"I know it is also what the Catholics believe," Lorena said, "and they draw their Power not only from their Priests but from their holy images."

As if she felt that the Duke was waiting for an explanation, she went on,

"I have seen them so often in Rome kneeling in front of a statue of one of their Saints or a holy painting, and I knew they were not only praying for help or for something they particularly desired but they felt that they were receiving some special Power from the object they were praying to."

"I understand what you are saying and it interests me enormously. On my travels I have often wondered what the Catholics, who I have seen lighting candles and praying in their Churches, were doing. Now you have explained it to me."

"I suppose," Lorena answered, "that somebody as important as you with so many people depending upon you needs more Power than someone as young and insignificant as myself."

"Are you suggesting that I should pray more fervently than anyone else?" the Duke asked in a slightly cynical voice.

"You don't need to pray as much as I must do," Lorena replied. "At the same time there is nobody who does not need to link up with the force and the Power of God. Even Christ had to do that."

The Duke thought that, if the house party could overhear this conversation taking place between him and a girl of eighteen, they would not believe it.

He could not remember talking about God and prayer with anybody since he was a child.

At Oxford University he and his friends had sometimes analysed their impulses and their actions and discussed in a somewhat abstract manner the difference between various religions.

But now, listening to Lorena, he thought that she made the whole of living seem simple and yet he knew how laughable his friends would find it.

It was so easy to mock her beliefs, to make a joke of the contention that a man like himself could draw his power from God.

He wondered if he should warn her to be careful with whom she discussed such things. Then he told himself that there was a purity and an innocent sincerity about her that any decent man would respect.

But he knew that this theory did not include women, especially a woman like Daisy.

It suddenly struck him that Daisy was not a good woman in any way. She was bad and for the first time in many years he questioned his own interest in a woman who had few of the characteristics that he really admired.

They had almost reached the front door before Lorena turned and said in a small voice,

"I am – sorry if what I have said has – bored you. Mama always said one must never – thrust one's own opinions on – other people."

"You have not thrust on me anything that I was not extremely interested to hear," the Duke replied.

He knew by her smile that his answer had pleased her.

Then the door of the carriage was opened and the drive was over.

*

Lorena spent a happy morning with Sir Hugo looking round the stables.

He told her that it was expected at Mere, as it was in most large houses, that on Sunday morning the guests should visit the stables.

The grooms had certainly gone to a great deal of trouble in preparing for them, Lorena noticed.

The passages had been freshly sanded, there was a straw plait to edge each stall and the horses had been brushed and groomed until their coats shone like satin.

Lorena and Sir Hugo had not been at the stables for long before they were joined by Lord Carnforth, who was talking about his own horses, Perry Gillingham, and three other members of the house party.

"You are up bright and early, Miss Benson," Lord Dartford addressed Lorena.

She was going to reply that she had been up a long time because she had been to Church, but then she thought it might sound as if she was being critical of those who had not attended the Service, so she merely smiled and replied,

"It is too lovely a day to stay in bed."

"I agree with you, but we were all too late last night pursuing Lady Luck, who certainly turned her back on me!"

"Did you lose a great deal of money?" Lorena asked sympathetically.

"More than I could afford," he replied.

She looked at him in a puzzled fashion and after a moment he said,

"I know you are thinking that I am a fool and that is what I am thinking myself. Like all gamblers I am always certain that the next card I turn up will win me a fortune."

"I read once," Lorena said, "that the odds against anyone who plays continually being an overall winner at the card tables are enormous."

"You are telling me what I already know! As I have told you, I am a fool, but perhaps in such company I am too proud to admit that I cannot really afford to play for such high stakes."

"It is wrong that you should be expected to do so," Lorena commented. "I do think if I was the Duke I would – "

She had no chance to say more for at that moment a voice behind her asked,

"Did I hear you say 'if I was the Duke'? I would be interested to hear the end of that sentence."

"If you had not interrupted, Alstone," Lord Dartford interposed before Lorena could reply, "you would have heard what Miss Benson had to say and actually I think it would have been sheer common sense."

"I am listening," the Duke continued.

"I would not like – you to think that I was – criticising," Lorena said quickly. "It was – only an idea."

The Duke's lips twisted.

"Another?" he said. "What is it this time?"

Lorena looked at Lord Dartford as if for permission to repeat what he had said.

"All right," he said with a smile, "tell the Duke if you want to. It will not do any harm for him to know the truth."

"The truth about what, Lionel?" the Duke enquired.

"Miss Benson will tell you that."

"What I was – saying," Lorena responded in a rather small voice, "was that if I was – Your Grace, I would not – allow people to – lose in my home more than they could really afford."

She saw the look of incredulity in the Duke's eyes.

"Not because I think gambling is – wrong," she went on, "although I don't understand why it has such an attraction for some people – it is simply because I would want – my guests to be happy."

Both of the men she was speaking to were listening to her intently and she went on,

"No one can be happy if he feels, as this gentleman does – that he has been very – foolish in losing so much – money in a game in which he had really little – chance of winning."

She stopped speaking and saw that the Duke was astounded.

Then he asked,

"Is this the truth, Lionel?"

"I am afraid it is."

"I realised that Arthur was making a killing last night, but I hoped that you had the sense to stop before you were seriously involved."

"You must blame your good wines for giving me a false optimism," Lord Dartford replied.

The Duke was frowning.

"I think Miss Benson is right. High stakes should be kept for the Clubs and not permitted in private houses where it is difficult for guests to break up a table or go to bed sooner than anyone else. I blame myself for letting this happen."

"No, *no*!" Lord Dartford cried. "You must not do that. It is entirely my own fault that I made a fool of myself. I cannot imagine why I bothered Miss Benson with my troubles. Let's go and look at the horses."

As he spoke, he turned away abruptly and walked into the stables.

Lorena looked up at the Duke.

"I am – sorry for – him."

"I will put things right somehow," the Duke replied. "You are not to worry about it."

"I will try not to," Lorena replied, "but – "

"I told you to leave everything to me," the Duke interrupted, "Let's go and look at the horses too."

He walked to the stables as he spoke and joined several others who were admiring the stallion he had ridden yesterday morning.

Lorena went to her uncle's side and after a moment, when they had moved into another stall and were out of earshot of the others, he enquired,

"What were you talking to Lord Dartford about?"

"He is upset because he lost a great deal of money last night," Lorena explained.

"So did a number of others," Sir Hugo replied, "but they are too sporting to whine about it."

"He was not whining," Lorena retorted. "He was just admitting to me that he had been very foolish."

"I see you are always prepared to support the underdog."

"But of course. Those at the top don't need any help, least of all from me!"

Her uncle laughed and then the conversation turned to horses and it was difficult to think of anything else.

It was nearly luncheontime before they had walked back to the house and Lorena, having tidied herself, came down to the Blue Drawing Room, where she knew they were to congregate.

Most of the house party was there and they all had glasses of champagne in their hands as she entered.

Her uncle was at the far end of the room and she had started to walk towards him when the Countess of Hellingford detached herself from the people she had been talking to and turned to face her.

She was looking, Lorena thought, exceedingly beautiful in a very elaborate gown of chiffon and lace, with five ropes of pearls round her neck and diamond earrings that glittered with every movement she made.

Lorena looked at her and smiled in admiration. Then, as she saw the expression in the Countess's eyes and realised that she was about to speak to her, she stopped still.

"I understand, Miss Benson," the Countess said in a voice that was clear enough to be heard by everybody in the room and which also had a note of almost icy venom in it, "that you accompanied His Grace to Church this morning. Surely, ignorant though you may be, you are nevertheless aware that it is not correct for an unmarried girl to go driving alone with a man?"

It seemed to Lorena that everyone in the room was suddenly silent as the Countess's voice rang out as accusingly as if she was standing in the dock.

For a moment she was too surprised to reply and then she answered,

"I am sorry – I don't think of His Grace – as being a man."

It was the childlike innocent way that she spoke that prevented those who were listening from finding anything funny in what she had said.

Then, before the Countess could answer, Sir Hugo came to the rescue.

"If, Daisy, I had realised how conscious *you* are of the *proprieties*, I would, of course, have accompanied Lorena to Church to see that she did not do anything so outrageous as to share a hymn book with Alstone or wave at a choirboy!"

The mocking way that Sir Hugo spoke and the way he accentuated the words '*you*' and '*proprieties*' made everybody laugh and there was no doubt that they were glad to relieve the tension by doing so.

But the Countess was not to be defeated.

"If you cannot look after your niece properly, Hugo," she said, "I am sure that Kitty will be only too willing to oblige when she returns from her little trip to Suffolk or was it actually Dorset that drew her?"

This, everybody knew, was a spiteful reference to Kitty's latest admirer, whose name was Lord Dorset.

Lorena did not understand, but everybody else in the room understood that Daisy was hitting back at Hugo not only for what he had said but for having a niece who had engaged the Duke's attention, if only for the time they had been in Church.

"How fortunate you are," Sir Hugo retorted, "that, unlike Kitty, your journey need not take you any farther than Mere!"

Again there was laughter.

A wordy duel between two members of the Windlemere Set was always amusing and far more entertaining than any drama that took place in the theatre.

"Daisy will be out for Hugo's blood after this!" somebody remarked in a low voice.

"And for the girl's," came a reply.

Sir Hugo put his arm round Lorena's shoulders.

"I am not going to offer you a glass of champagne," he said, "as I think you would not care for it at this hour of the morning, but I am sure you would enjoy a non-alcoholic drink, apple juice for instance."

"That – would be – lovely."

Lorena stumbled a little over the words, knowing that, although it was stupid of her, she felt shaken by the way that the Countess had spoken to her and by the animosity in her eyes.

'I wonder why she hates me,' she ruminated and could find no explanation.

Only when she went in to luncheon and saw the Countess talking to the Duke did she understand.

Lorena thought that she must have been blind not to realise it before and she knew that she had told the truth when she had said that she did not think of the Duke as a man.

Of course he was a man, in fact he is the most attractive handsome man she could ever imagine. But she supposed that, because he was so magnificent and so exactly what she had hoped for, she had thought of him as being like a King or a God in Ancient Greece – omnipotent and not human.

He had been so kind to her, letting her ride with him, driving her back from Church, but all the time they had talked together it had never crossed her mind that she was with what her mother would have called 'a young man'.

She remembered hearing her mother say in the past,

"I know, darling, when you grow up there will be lots of young men to admire you and who will want to dance with you. I hope one day you will meet a young man with whom you will fall in love as I fell in love with your father."

'Mama was 'in love' with Papa.'

Lorena thought the words beneath her breath and she knew that what the Countess felt for the Duke was love. She was 'in love' with him and was jealous because he had been to Church with somebody else.

It was ridiculous, of course, but Lorena knew from her books that jealousy caused people to behave violently like Othello in Shakespeare's tragic play.

'It was – wrong of me to drive with him – alone,' she thought to herself.

She had suggested that she should walk home, but how could she explain that to the Countess?

Then she remembered that the Countess had a husband.

Her uncle had mentioned him, wondering how many lions he had shot in Africa.

He had not been talking to her, but to several other people and the Marchioness of Trumpington had said,

"There is one lioness he should have taken with him or shot before he left!"

There was a burst of laughter at this, but Lorena had not understood. Now she thought that the Marchioness must have been referring to the Countess of Hellingford.

'Perhaps I ought to explain to her,' Lorena thought, 'that I did not mean to go driving with the Duke and I do not think of him as a young man in the same way that she does.'

Then she asked herself if that was quite true.

Now that she thought about it, the Duke was very much a man and no doubt that was really why she had enjoyed being with him and it would be very, very disappointing if she could never be with him in the same way again.

It had been so exciting to ride alone with him and it had been even more thrilling when they had breakfasted together and talked in the farmhouse.

He seemed to understand what she was trying to say and it suddenly struck her that of all the men in the party, even her uncle, the Duke was the one person who would not laugh at her 'ideas' as he called them.

'I like him. I like him very much!' Lorena thought to herself.

It seemed unfair that the Countess should wish to keep him all to herself.

Lorena wondered whether, if she was in love with a man, especially with one as handsome as the Duke, she would be jealous too and rude to other women simply because he had talked to them.

"You are very silent," ventured Kelvin Fane.

Once again he was sitting next to her at a meal.

"What are you thinking about?"

Because Lorena felt that she knew him and, without considering what she should say, she told the truth.

"I was thinking about the Duke."

"I suggest you think about somebody else," he said, "unless you want Daisy to scratch your eyes out!"

Lorena was still for a moment and then she asked,

"Is she – very much in – love with him?"

"She thinks she is."

"A-and – the Duke?"

"That is a question he should answer for himself. Anyway it is much the best for you not to concern yourself with his affairs."

"Yes – of course."

Lorena felt humbly that it had been presumptuous of her to ask the questions that she had already asked.

"You are much too young to be at a party like this," Major Fane remarked sharply.

"I appreciate that everybody here is – older than – I am," Lorena answered, "but I am trying not to be a – nuisance when Uncle Hugo has been so – kind as to bring me."

"You are not in the least a nuisance," Major Fane replied. "The only trouble is that you are out of your depth and you may get hurt in the process of trying to swim to safety."

"Why – should I be – hurt?"

She thought Major Fane was going to give her an explanation, but then he obviously changed his mind.

"I will tell you another time, but if you take my advice, you will leave the Duke alone."

He paused before he asked her,

"Do you promise to do that?"

"I will – try," Lorena answered.

Even as she spoke, she knew that it was something that she did not wish to do.

She liked the Duke and wanted to be with him.

CHAPTER FIVE

After luncheon, as if he wanted to make up to her for the uncomfortable feeling caused by the Countess, Sir Hugo suggested to Lorena that they should go riding.

She enjoyed their ride, although she felt slightly guilty when her uncle spoke to her as if it was the first time that she had been on one of the Duke's horses.

Too late she felt that she should have told him what she had been doing yesterday morning when she came back to Mere.

But, because she had already had breakfast in the farmhouse and therefore did not need another one, she had not met her uncle until later in the morning.

As he was with a number of other people, there seemed to be no point in drawing attention to herself by saying that she had been riding with the Duke.

"I should have remembered yesterday that you would like to ride," Sir Hugo said after they had galloped over the parkland. "But make quite sure while you are here that you take every opportunity of enjoying the Duke's outstanding horses.

It was strange, Lorena thought, but she could not help feeling disappointed, or was it depressed, at the thought that she would not be able to ride again alone with the Duke.

Looking back on her first ride early in the morning when the mist was on the lake and she and the Duke had galloped for a long time before they spoke to each other, it had been an enchantment that she could not put into words.

Then they had talked together in the farmhouse and he had been so understanding and she thought now that she should have realised at the time that it was too wonderful an experience to be repeated.

Sir Hugo interrupted her thoughts by saying as their horses moved side-by-side,

"Are you enjoying yourself, Lorena?"

"Very, very much, Uncle Hugo."

"I am sorry that things were somewhat awkward this morning, but Daisy is a very difficult woman."

Lorena did not reply and after a moment he went on,

"As, of course, you are well aware, it is wrong for any lady to make scenes in such a manner and she certainly had no right to attack you for doing nothing more reprehensible than going to Church. But you will find, when you have lived in the world as long as I have, that one has to take these things as they come."

Lorena gave a little laugh.

"That is what my Nanny used to say when I was a child."

"It is quite a good motto for all of us," Sir Hugo said, "and my Nanny used to say, 'never expect too much, so you won't be disappointed'."

Lorena laughed.

"I am sure that mine said the same. She was full of wise sayings and, sometimes when I remember them now, they are helpful."

"I want to say," Sir Hugo pointed out, as if he was following the train of his own thoughts, "that I am very proud of the way you have behaved. I am aware how difficult it must be for a girl to be pitchforked straight from school into a party at Mere, where everyone knows everybody else. But you have managed most successfully."

"Thank you, Uncle Hugo. It is very kind of you to say that."

"Sometime we must have a talk about your future," Sir Hugo went on, "but not until the end of the week when we have to leave. I want you to relax and enjoy yourself."

Lorena could not help a little tremor of fear and she was certain from the way he spoke that what he would tell her at the end of the week would not be good news.

'What will happen to me?' she pondered. 'Where will I go? Who shall I be with?'

It struck her almost despairingly that the one person she might never see again would be the Duke.

She had promised Major Fane that she would try to leave the Duke alone, but she could not help thinking of him and later in the afternoon it was impossible to do anything else.

~123~

When she and her uncle rode back to Mere, he told her he was going to play bridge and Lorena therefore went in search of Mr. Ashley.

Surprisingly, although it was Sunday, she found that he was in his office.

"Perhaps I ought not to ask you today of all days," she began, "but could you show me some more of the house?"

"I should be delighted to do so, Miss Benson," he replied. "When His Grace is in residence, Sunday is the same as any other day to me."

He took Lorena round the Picture Gallery, the Orangery, the library and then a number of State Reception rooms where Robert Adam had designed not only the walls and ceilings but also the glorious gold furniture, which made Lorena think once again that Mere was a Fairytale Palace.

When they came to what Mr. Ashley told Lorena was called the Silver Sitting Room, she saw there some more modern paintings than in the other rooms and these included a recent one of the Duke resplendent in the robes he had worn at the Coronation of King George V.

Lorena stood looking at it, feeling, because it was so well painted, almost as if she could talk to him as she had done this morning when they drove back to Mere from Church.

Then Mr. Ashley said,

"The sketch over the mantelpiece by John Sargent is of the Duchess on her Wedding Day."

Lorena looked at him in astonishment.

"The Duchess?"

"The Duke was married. Did you not know that?"

"I had no idea."

"It was twelve years ago, when His Grace was just twenty-one and the Duchess was killed in a fall out hunting before they had been married a year."

"How terrible!" Lorena exclaimed.

Then, because she could not help herself, she asked,

"Was – His Grace very – upset?"

"It was a tragedy for everyone concerned," Mr. Ashley replied. "Now, let me show you these children's paintings by Hoppner, which are considered to be very fine examples of his work."

Lorena sensed that Mr. Ashley did not wish to speak any further about the Duchess. At the same time she found it very hard to take in anything else that the curator was saying.

The Duke had been *married!*

She did not know why, but it was quite a shock.

It had never occurred to her that he had had a wife at Mere and that he was a widower.

Perhaps, she thought, he had been desperately unhappy at losing her and very lonely and that was why he filled his life with friends who were witty and amusing and kept him entertained.

'I know so little about him,' she thought to herself.

Before they left the Silver Sitting Room her eyes went back again to the Duke's portrait, thinking that the artist had captured his look of aloofness and also the impression he conveyed of being imperious and overwhelming.

It was difficult to gauge what the Duchess had been like, except that she was attractive with black hair and large dark eyes.

'Perhaps he only likes black-haired women,' Lorena thought.

Then she remembered that the Countess of Hellingford was certainly not dark but fair and very Junoesque.

'I am small and insignificant beside her and also the Duchess,' Lorena murmured to herself.

Then she remembered that she was breaking her promise to Major Fane.

'He will never know it,' she excused herself, 'nor will the Duke.'

But when she was dressed for dinner, she could not help hoping that she would not look too unattractive in comparison with the beautiful guests whom she had described to the Duke as looking like 'swans gliding over a lake'.

She was certain that they would, each of them, wear a gown that they had not worn before, their jewels would be spectacular and the things that they would say would amuse the Duke and the gentlemen whom they sat next to at dinner, as she was unable to do.

'Major Fane is right,' she thought as she looked in the mirror. 'I am too young and it is only out of kindness to Uncle Hugo that anyone even speaks to me.'

Because she had only two evening gowns, tonight she put on the one that she had worn the night she had arrived.

It had seemed so attractive when she had chosen it in Rome.

Now she thought it was too plain and she wished that she could be covered with the frills of tulle and swirls of chiffon and especially the glittering jewels that made the other women shine like stars in the sky.

A knock on her door interrupted her thoughts and, when Emily went to open it, she thought despairingly that not even flowers could make her look anything but a schoolgirl.

Emily came to her side to say,

"Look, miss. There's no choice tonight, as His Grace has sent these specially for you."

"Especially for me?" Lorena repeated.

Her heart gave a sudden jump as he had thought of her, because he had been kind enough to remember that she would have no diamonds or emeralds and no rubies or sapphires to brighten her appearance.

Instead on the tray there was a corsage of orchids and what appeared to be a wreath of them to wear on her head.

They were not in the least like the orchids that she had worn on the first night. These were very pale pink and different from any flowers Lorena had ever seen before.

"They're ever so beautiful, miss," Emily piped up. "They must be some of the rare species that His Grace grows in the Orchid House. My father's one of the gardeners who looks after them and he says His Grace has them sent from all sorts of outlandish places all over the world."

"These are certainly incredibly beautiful," Lorena commented. "And there is a wreath for my hair!"

"Yes, miss, and if you like, I'll pin it at the back of your head like one of them tiaras they wears in Russia."

Lorena knew what she meant and asked with a smile,

"Have you seen a tiara?"

"Yes, miss. There was a Princess stayin' here last year and, when she came to dinner, she wore a tiara that were an arch over the top of her head and that's what these orchids can do for you."

Lorena thought they certainly made her look quite different and the pale pink of the flowers seemed to transform the severity of her gown so that it made a perfect foil for them.

She pinned the corsage low down between her breasts and, when she looked at her reflection in the mirror, she knew that her eyes were shining and she was no longer afraid of seeming small and insignificant.

He had thought of her!

He had sent her the flowers, but she must never say so in case it made the Countess angry.

There was another knock at the door and Sir Hugo came into the room.

"You are ready, my dear?" he asked. "We must not be late."

"Yes, Uncle Hugo. I am ready."

"That is a very pretty wreath you have on your head – " he began, then he stopped and exclaimed,

"They are real! I thought when I came into the room that the flowers must be artificial."

"No, they are real," Lorena replied.

"They are certainly more attractive than any flowers I have seen for a long time," Sir Hugo said. "Well, come along, my dear, or I shall be too late to have a drink before dinner."

They walked down the staircase, Lorena hoping that nobody else would think it strange that she was wearing such beautiful flowers.

She was not only afraid that, if they did, the Countess would be angry, but she thought somehow that even to discuss them might spoil the joy she felt

~129~

because the Duke had taken the trouble to send them to her.

Fortunately everybody in the Blue Drawing Room was too engrossed in conversation to notice her, except, although she may have been mistaken, she thought that the Duke glanced in her direction and then away again.

A hand touched hers and the Marchioness of Trumpington drew her to one side.

"I am sorry, dear child," she began, "if you were upset by Daisy's being so unkind before luncheon. Had I known that you wished to go to Church, I would have gone with you."

"That would have been very kind of you," Lorena smiled, "but I did not want to be a trouble to anybody."

"No, of course not, and that is the last thing you are," the Marchioness said reassuringly. "Daisy is absurdly jealous of anybody who even speaks to the Duke and, being pretty as you are, always has its penalties."

"I certainly do not feel pretty when I look at you," Lorena declared in all sincerity.

The Marchioness was looking very beautiful in a gown of Nile-blue tulle that accentuated the red of her hair.

She wore a necklace and a small tiara of aquamarines, which had just become fashionable and a bracelet of the same stones on her wrist.

She smiled at the compliment, but before she could reply, Lord Gilmour joined them, saying,

"Daisy is showing off like a peacock with two tails! But, as far as I am concerned, there is only one beautiful woman in the room and that is you, Enid!"

There was a note in his voice that made Lorena look at him in surprise.

Then, as she saw the expression in his eyes, she drew in her breath.

Lord Gilmour was in love with the Marchioness of Trumpington!

But then she was sure that they both were married.

She felt bewildered and, when they went in to dinner she looked up and down the table, wondering how many of the men present were in love with women who were not their wives.

She saw that once again the Countess of Hellingford was making every effort to capture the Duke's attention and the Marchioness, with a very soft expression in her eyes, was listening to what Lord Gilmour was saying.

Opposite her the Viscountess Storr was having an obviously intimate and very personal quarrel with Major Fane.

She was pouting and shrugging her shoulders and he was frowning, obviously put out by what she was saying.

Lorena's eyes rested for a moment on her uncle.

He at least did not seem to be engaged particularly with any of the ladies present.

Then she remembered the tone that the Countess of Hellingford had used when referring to her Aunt Kitty,

"Or was it actually *Dorset* that drew her?"

It was only after luncheon that Lorena understood that the Countess had been referring not to the County of that name but to a person.

She had not even been aware that there was someone called 'Lord Dorset' until just before they were going riding, when she heard her uncle say to his valet,

"This is not my whip. Mine has a gold band round it."

The valet looked at it.

"I'm ever so sorry, sir," he said apologetically. "I picked it up in a hurry when we were packin' to come here, and I must have brought his Lordship's instead of yours."

"Then see that it is returned to Lord Dorset as soon as we return to London," Sir Hugo said sharply. "And another time don't be so careless."

"I'm very sorry, sir," the valet said again.

At the time Lorena had thought that her uncle seemed unnecessarily put out until she realised that the name rang a bell.

It was all very complicated, she thought and then, almost like the pieces of a puzzle falling into place, she began to understand some of the things that had worried her.

Aunt Kitty and Lord Dorset!

No wonder there was no place for her in her uncle's house in Belgrave Square or for that matter at his home in the country.

She found herself remembering how her father had talked of the Marriage Service as a Sacrament, sacred and Holy and, of course, the vows that the bride and bridegroom had taken could never be broken.

Once her father had come home looking upset and her mother had asked him,

"What is the matter, darling? What is troubling you?"

"It's the Wedding I have just officiated at," her father replied. "I felt that the whole atmosphere was wrong and there was not a genuine prayer or act of faith in the whole Church."

"Perhaps you were mistaken."

Her father shook his head.

"No, I could feel it vividly. I knew that the bride was marrying the bridegroom for his money and he was content with the deal because his bride moves in a higher social circle than the one he was born into."

Lorena's mother had risen from the table to kiss her husband and say,

"You must not take these things to heart, dearest." Lorena heard her father laugh and saw how cleverly her mother had been able to spirit away his depression.

There had been many other occasions when he had believed that he had joined together two people who would find happiness because they were meant for each other.

Wealth, circumstance and social position had no importance for him, it was only love that counted.

"I really like the Marriage Service to be one of dedication and a union of love," Lorena's father had said positively.

"Like ours," her mother had pointed out softly, "and that is how it will be when you marry young Wilcox tomorrow. I have never known two people more in love. I always thought that she was rather a plain girl, but now she is almost a beauty!"

Looking back Lorena realised that the people who felt like this were usually humble people, young men and women who lived in the village or others who were more well to do but did not aspire to any great social heights.

'Perhaps money corrupts,' she thought.

Then she told herself that, if the person who possessed money had the right sort of character and high ideals, then no amount of it could really change or destroy them.

Then she rebuked herself for being selfish and thinking about herself instead of trying to entertain the gentlemen on either side of her at the dinner table.

She turned to the man on her right and tried to find out what was his particular interest. She managed to have quite interesting conversations with both her partners before the elaborate seven course meal came to an end.

After dinner in the drawing room, Lorena was wise enough to go at once to the Marchioness of Trumpington's side, who smiled at her.

"I wonder," Lorena asked her, "if I could play the piano? If I played very softly, it would not interrupt anything that anyone was saying."

The Marchioness guessed that she was afraid of becoming involved with the Countess and she said at once,

"It would be a very good idea and I would like to hear you play. I feel sure that you had a good teacher in Rome."

"An Italian whose music was his whole life," Lorena replied.

As she spoke, she went to the piano that stood in an alcove.

It was a magnificent Broadway and, as Lorena sat down and her hands touched the keys, she knew that she might never again have the opportunity of playing on such a fine instrument.

But that, of course, was on a par with everything else at Mere.

She chose first the quiet music of Chopin. She was determined not to give the Countess a chance to find fault and claim that she was interrupting their conversations.

Tonight Daisy Hellingford was looking not only beautiful but spectacular and she was obviously holding court amongst the other ladies.

She was 'queening it' over them as if by right of the position, Lorena thought, which she assumed was because she loved the Duke and he loved her.

It gave Lorena a strange pain to think of it, although why it should, she had no idea.

It was the same feeling, she realised, that she had experienced when she learnt that the Duke had been married.

Then she told herself that it was just imagination and began to concentrate almost fiercely on what she was playing.

From Chopin her fingers turned to the romantic music of Offenbach and then, as the gentlemen entered the drawing room, she felt that there was no need for her to continue to play and that she was now safe from the Countess.

As she saw the Duke walking down the room towards the ladies grouped at the far end of it, she rose from the piano and, moving swiftly, slipped out through the nearest French window onto the terrace outside.

It was a very warm night without a breath of wind, the stars bejewelled the sky and there was a moon throwing its light over the garden and making the lake look silver and magical.

Without planning where she would go, Lorena walked along the terrace in her satin slippers, descended some steps onto the lawn and moved away from the house.

It seemed ridiculous, now that she was free of it, that she should have been afraid of anyone, but she knew she did not want the Countess of Hellingford to spoil the enchantment she had felt ever since she had come to Mere.

Already it was as if part of the dream had been torn aside and she was seeing and hearing things that she had not noticed before and what she had learnt was detracting from the beauty that had held her spellbound.

'It's just like waking up,' Lorena thought, 'when I want to go on dreaming.'

She felt as if the Fairytale was slipping away from her and all she would be left with was a reality that might be ugly and unpleasant.

The loveliness of the garden was like a cool hand on a fevered brow.

Whatever was happening in the brilliantly lit drawing room she had left behind her, here was peace, the quiet and the wonder of the night.

There was the fragrance of the night-scented stock, the shrill squeak of an occasional bat overhead and there was the moon, the stars and the feeling that she was surrounded by friendly beings from another world although she could not see them.

'Perhaps,' Lorena thought, 'they are the people who have lived at Mere, who once walked in the garden as I am doing to escape from their troubles and difficulties.'

Perhaps too, she thought, there were also celestial beings round her, who could move amongst mortals and influence them to seek for something higher than themselves, something that was definitely there but just out of reach.

By the time Lorena reached the water lily pool, which was surrounded by a yew hedge on which there were strange and skilfully cut examples of topiary work, she was lost in her imagination, happy in a way that was impossible to describe.

With each step everything disturbing fell away and she became transformed because her whole being was uplifted spiritually.

In the centre of the water lily pond was a carved statue of Eros holding in his arms a large fish from whose mouth poured a stream of water into the pool beneath him.

The moonlight made him silvery and very enticing, and there was only the soft fall of the water and the stars reflected on it.

Lorena looked up and felt as though something within her, perhaps her heart, flowed up to the sky and gave her the Power that she had spoken to the Duke about, the Power that she knew came from God and was His.

Then she heard footsteps coming towards her along the path that had brought her to the water lily pool.

For a moment she drew in her breath, hoping, with a hope that she could not repress, that it was the Duke who had come to join her.

But instead in the moonlight she saw Major Fane.

*

The Duke had been well aware when he reached the end of the drawing room that Lorena had disappeared through the French windows out onto the terrace.

He could understand that she wanted to get away and, when he had come into the drawing room, he had actually been relieved to find that she was nowhere near Daisy.

He wondered who had suggested to her that she might play the piano and thought perhaps it was Enid Trumpington. But he knew that it would be unwise for him to ask questions.

"Are you going to gamble, Alstone?" Daisy asked.

She was good-tempered tonight and the Duke was not certain whether it was because she thought that she had won a battle or because he, to save Lorena from her sharp tongue, had gone out of his way to be pleasant to her.

"Of course," he replied. "I thought that was what you would want."

"I won a little money last night," Daisy told him, "but not enough. You must sit near me, Alstone, and bring me luck."

"I must see what my other guests wish to do first," he said. "You go to the big table and get it organised, you always do that so well."

Daisy smiled.

She was always delighted when the Duke treated her as if she was the hostess at Mere, which was most definitely what she wanted to be.

'He is mine,' she thought to herself, 'and the sooner everybody realises that I can prevent them from being invited here if I wish to the better!'

It was a pretence that she knew had no substance in fact, but Daisy could always believe what she wanted to believe.

As she settled everybody into their places at the baccarat table, she did so in a manner that made it quite obvious that she was running the show her way and was the only one who counted.

Three of the guests wanted to play bridge and the Duke had just found them a fourth player when he noticed that Kelvin Fane was not at the baccarat table as he had expected but was walking through the open window onto the terrace.

The Duke was instantly aware that he was following Lorena and he thought with a sudden irritation that it was too bad of Fane after Daisy's behaviour before luncheon to put the girl in danger of evoking a scene with Sarah Storr.

'This is the last time I shall ever invite a young unmarried girl to one of my parties,' he vowed to himself.

Then it struck him that it was not because Lorena was young-and unmarried that she was causing trouble amongst his guests but because she had an attraction that was unusual.

Whatever it might be, he was responsible for the girl and Fane had no right to be alone with her in the garden, which would certainly infuriate Sarah and cause a great deal of comment, even if it was good-natured, from everyone else.

Therefore at a moment when Daisy was busily engaged in dealing the cards, he went out onto the terrace and wondered in which direction Lorena had gone.

He was sure, although he did not know why, that she would find her way to the water lily pool in the garden.

It was one of the loveliest of the small gardens that had been laid out by his grandmother and even as a small boy he had found it particularly attractive.

There was also a Herb Garden surrounded by red brick Elizabethan walls, there was a Rose garden that had a sundial in the centre of it and there was a Japanese Garden where all the trees and shrubs were tiny dwarves of their much larger species.

There were other gardens farther away from the house, but the nearest was the water lily garden and the Duke thought that it was one of the most beautiful.

He moved quickly over the soft lawn and then, as he neared the garden, he knew that he had been right in his assumption for he heard voices.

His first impulse was to join Lorena and Kelvin Fane.

Then, as he reached the yew hedge, he was aware that he could hear what they were saying.

"It is very lovely here," Lorena said, "but I think we ought to go back to the house."

"There is no hurry," Kelvin Fane replied. "Everybody is playing bridge or baccarat and I want to talk to you."

"What – about?"

"Yourself."

"I can only think how lovely the water lily garden is."

"You are lovely too!"

"I think we – should go back."

There was no doubt that Lorena was nervous and the Duke reached out his hands to part the branches of the yew hedge in front of him.

Through the space he made he could see her quite clearly standing by the little pool with the moonlight lighting her face, while Kelvin Fane had his back to him.

"I will take you back," Kelvin offered, "but first, because like you I find everything here so beautiful, I want to kiss you. You have never been kissed, Lorena, and I want to be the first."

"No!"

Lorena had not moved, but she spoke positively.

"No?" Kelvin Fane questioned. "Why should you say that?"

"Because when I am – kissed, I think – perhaps it might be very – wonderful but I would like the – man I kissed to be the man I would marry."

There was a silence and the Duke knew that Kelvin Fane was surprised.

"I think," he said after a moment, "that you might find it difficult to know if you wish to marry a man unless you have kissed him first."

Lorena shook her head before she stated,

"You may think it foolish of me – but I am sure that if I loved someone enough to want to – marry him – I would know it in my heart."

"Perhaps you are right, but I still want to kiss you, Lorena. I want it more than I have wanted anything for a long time."

The Duke had the feeling that he was going to insist and he thought angrily that this was something he could not allow.

He was ready to walk down the steps into the garden and interrupt Fane before he had time to frighten Lorena, but before he could do so he heard her say,

"I think that, if the lady who – loves you heard you say such things to me, she would be angry and I would not blame her because it is surely disloyal to love one woman and want to kiss another."

If Lorena had surprised Fane before, she had certainly succeeded in astonishing him now, the Duke thought.

"I am a free man," Fane said, as if he must excuse himself. "I belong to nobody, Lorena, and no one can stop me from wanting to kiss you. And nor is it disloyal."

"Then if it is not disloyal," Lorena replied, "it is unkind. I don't want to be unkind to anyone – and please – I do *not* want to be kissed."

There was something in the way she spoke, the little tremor in her voice and the fact that in the moonlight she looked so lovely and yet so fragile.

She might in fact have been no older than the boy Eros standing in the centre of the water lily pond and, as if she had used a weapon far more effective than the arrows Eros carried on his shoulder, Kelvin Fane capitulated.

"I will not do anything you would not wish me to, Lorena, but will you promise me something?"

"Another promise?" Lorena enquired.

"The promise I extracted from you at luncheon was to save you from getting hurt by becoming involved with our host. What I am going to ask you now is something quite different."

"What is it?"

She was still a little nervous and still afraid, the Duke thought apprehensively, because she was now aware, as she might not have been before, that Kelvin Fane was a man and he desired something else.

"What I am going to ask you is that, when we leave Mere, I can see you. It is, as you have probably noticed, a little difficult here, and elsewhere it would be very different. I want to see you again, Lorena, more than I can tell you."

"I would like to see you again," Lorena answered, "but I don't know where I shall be or where I am to live."

"That is immaterial," Kelvin Fane said. "I will find you. Then, Lorena, we can really get to know each other as I would like to do."

There was a note of urgency in his voice that made Lorena say again,

"I think we should go back."

She could not proceed down the path unless he stepped out of her way.

She took a hesitating step forward, then for a moment their eyes met and the Duke, watching, was still, aware that it was a battle of wills.

It was strange, he thought, that anyone so young and so inexperienced as Lorena could fight one of the most experienced and certainly the most ardent lover in the Social world.

And yet, as he waited, almost holding his breath to see the result, Lorena won.

Kelvin Fane stepped to one side and she passed him and then he walked after her down the narrow path that led out of the garden.

With a swiftness that was thanks to his athletic ability, the Duke moved away from the yew hedge and by the time Lorena and Kelvin Fane emerged onto the lawn he was advancing towards them as if he was just coming from the house.

"There you are!" he exclaimed. "I came to tell you, Kelvin, that you are wanted at the baccarat table or rather I think they want your money!"

"Then they are not going to have it!" Kelvin Fane replied. "I have no intention of playing tonight and to tell the truth I am rather bored with baccarat. I will cut in at bridge, or, if you prefer, play you a game of piquet."

There had been a momentary start at seeing the Duke so near to them, but Kelvin Fane had spoken quite naturally.

Lorena had felt her heart leap with an irrepressible gladness as she saw the Duke coming towards them.

She had been afraid that Major Fane would insist on kissing her and she felt that it would be undignified and embarrassing to have to struggle against him.

She had never before been in such a position with a man and she had known when the Major had said that he wished to kiss her that she did not want him to and the words that she had refused him with had come to her mind almost as if they were an inspiration from outside herself.

Still she had been afraid, but now that she saw the Duke, so tall and so broad-shouldered, she had an impulse to run towards him and tell him how frightened she had been and how glad she was that he was there.

Then, as he joined them and they all three walked across the lawn back towards the lights gleaming golden from the windows onto the terrace, she knew that everything was wonderful again and her dream was still with her because the Duke was there too.

When they reached the terrace, the Duke deliberately stopped as they reached the light from the window to lean over the balustrade and look towards the lake.

"You had better go in, Kelvin," he suggested. "I will join you in a moment or two."

He knew as he spoke that Fane was an intelligent man and realised that for him to appear with Lorena would give both Sarah and Daisy something to be unpleasant about.

Accordingly Kelvin Fane walked in through the drawing room window and Lorena heard the Marchioness call out his name from the baccarat table.

"I think Mere is more beautiful by moonlight than at any other time," the Duke said conversationally to Lorena.

"I-I suppose it was – wrong of me to go alone into the garden," Lorena replied.

"Not wrong, perhaps unwise," the Duke answered.

"I am – sorry – I keep making mistakes."

"They are not really mistakes," the Duke said. "I do not want you to worry about them. What I want you to do is to go in now and play the piano very softly as you were doing when we joined you after dinner."

"I would love to. You don't think that I shall be interrupting anybody?"

"You will not interrupt those who are gaming and, as they will know where you are, there will be no reason to gossip about you."

"I understand – and it is very wise of you and once again I am – sorry I was so – foolish."

"When you have played enough," the Duke said, "you can either join us in the anteroom or, if you prefer, you can go to bed."

"That would not be rude?"

"No one will think it rude that you are not throwing your money away on what you say is an odds on chance that you will not win."

Lorena gave a little laugh.

"I would not gamble anyway, even if I had any money. I will go to bed and read. I found some very interesting books in your library this afternoon."

"I thought you would discover them sooner or later."

"I discovered other things as well and Mr. Ashley tells me that there are still more treasures for me to discover tomorrow."

"And when you have been everywhere, will you then be bored?" the Duke asked her.

"Never! I could never be bored here," Lorena said, "I believe that one is never bored with beautiful things, only perhaps sometimes with people."

He found some of the strange perceptive things she said so unexpected and she gave him a smile as she said,

"Goodnight, Your Grace, and thank you again so very, very much for – everything."

She slipped away from him as she spoke and went back through the open window into the now-deserted drawing room.

The Duke waited and after a moment there was a melody being played skilfully, he realised, by someone who loved music and had been well taught.

He listened to what she was playing and knew that it was actually a little paean of gratitude for what she had seen and found at Mere.

She could obviously translate quite easily into music what she was saying and thinking.

He listened for some minutes and then sauntered slowly into the anteroom.

Daisy saw him and called out,

"Alstone, where have you been? There is a place here for you."

The Duke walked across to the table and sat down in the chair next to hers.

"Where have you been?" she asked him again.

"Getting some fresh air," he answered. "I find it rather hot tonight."

He knew that by this explanation he allayed any suspicion that she might be feeling.

"You should have let me know," she countered automatically.

Then, as she dealt him the cards, she said, almost under her breath so that only he could hear,

"Darling, I missed you. You know I hate you to be away from me even for a few minutes."

The way she spoke made the Duke feel that she was reaching out her hands and holding onto him, holding him captive and striving to make him her prisoner.

He felt an unusual anger rising within him.

He had no wish to be tied and no wish to belong to any woman, whoever she might be.

Then he remembered overhearing Kelvin Fane saying that he was free and he knew that it was a lie.

They were none of them free.

These women were determined to hold them enthralled and the Duke was embroiled with Daisy as Lorena had known Kelvin was with Sarah.

'Dammit all,' he said to himself. 'Am I man or a mouse that I should let this happen to me?'

He looked at his cards and then flung them down on the table.

"I have no wish to play tonight," he asserted. "It's too hot."

He pushed back his chair and rose to his feet as Daisy gave a cry of protest.

"But, Alstone! This is – "

The Duke knew what she was saying, but he would not listen to it.

He walked across the room to where Kelvin Fane was standing with an obstinate look on his face, listening to Sarah Storr, who had risen from the table to speak to him.

"I don't know about you, Fane," the Duke said, "but I would like a game of billiards. Are you prepared to give me one?"

"Yes, of course," the Major replied. "That is what I call a sensible suggestion."

"I want you to play bridge with me," Sarah Storr protested.

"You have your four," Kelvin Fane replied.

The Duke had moved towards the door and the Major was following when Sarah Storr caught hold of his arm.

"Don't be too late," she said in a whisper. "I will be waiting for you, dearest."

Kelvin Fane did not reply.

He knew, as he walked towards the billiards room beside the Duke, that he would not see Sarah again that night.

CHAPTER SIX

The Duke was fast asleep when he was aroused by the growling of his dog, Rufus, who always slept with him.

It was unusual for Rufus to wake him during the night and, as the Duke opened his eyes, he thought that it must be morning.

Then he saw that the room was completely dark except that he had pulled back the curtains before he went to bed because it was so hot and he could then see the stars in the sky.

Rufus growled again and the Duke wondered what could be upsetting him.

Then the dog went to the door and sniffed.

Now the Duke was sure that somebody was outside in the passage and he wondered who it could be.

It was most unlikely that anyone would be passing his room, because he was in the Master suite, which, while on the first floor of the main building, was not near any of the other rooms except for one.

In that room slept the Countess, but it was most improbable that she should be moving about at this time of the night or coming to him.

He had not, as she had wished him to do, gone to her room last night when they had come up to bed.

He knew that she was waiting for him to do so, as she had waited the night before, but he had no inclination to go to her and she was experienced enough in the handling of men not to press him.

Nevertheless, when they had all gone up the stairs together after the baccarat was finished and the Duke's guests one by one had said 'goodnight' and gone to their own rooms, only Daisy had been left.

He had stopped outside her door.

"Goodnight, Daisy," he said. "I am glad you won tonight."

"Must it be 'goodnight'?" she enquired.

She looked very beautiful in the light from the gold sconces in the corridor and the Duke could not understand his feeling that he had no wish to touch her.

He was even reluctant to raise her hand to his lips although he felt obliged to do so.

'I am tired,' he muttered to himself.

As he spoke, he was ashamed of himself for giving such a banal reason, which he was sure that Daisy would know was untrue.

He did kiss her hand and as, feeling bewildered, she drew him a little towards her, he turned away.

"Goodnight, Daisy," he said. "It's very late, so I am sure you will sleep well."

He saw that she made a movement as if she would stop him, but he was moving away down the corridor to his own room and he did not look back.

Now, as Rufus went on sniffing at the door, the Duke listened and waited tensely.

He thought that it would be undignified and extremely embarrassing to have a scene with Daisy at this moment, but his door did not open.

Now he felt certain, although he was not sure why, that whoever it was had passed on down the corridor.

It suddenly struck him that there might be a burglar in the house.

There were always nightwatchmen on duty, but he had thought for some time that they were getting old and he was thinking about installing one of the new burglar alarms, which he had been told were extremely effective.

It had never seemed necessary to guard against burglars at Mere, but there had been talk lately of robbers breaking into various large houses and the Duke knew that the treasures he possessed could prove a great temptation to those who were known as 'collectors' and who often employed very dubious methods to add to their collections.

At last he sprang out of bed and, putting on his slippers and a long velvet robe that was laid on a chair, walked to the door.

Rufus was now growling as if he was still aware of an intruder but it was already becoming a memory and something of the past.

Feeling his way, as he did not wish to put on the light, the Duke found the handle of the door and turned it softly.

Outside in the passage, as was usual when everybody had retired to bed, the night-footmen had left only a few lights burning in each corridor.

The Duke advanced from his own room and thought, although he could not be certain, that in the shadows something moved at the far end of it.

Curious now and determined to investigate, he walked quickly towards the place where he thought that he had seen a movement and only as he reached it did he notice at the end of the corridor the small twisting staircase that led up to the roof.

It had been so long since he had gone any further along the corridor than to his own room that he had almost forgotten that the staircase existed.

Now he was certain that whoever had disturbed Rufus had gone up the staircase as if to hide.

It flashed through his mind that burglars would find the huge roofs of Mere a convenient place not only to hide but to descend to the ground at a different point from where they had come in and thus escaping observation.

As he moved swiftly up the staircase, he thought that perhaps he had been rather foolish in not bringing a weapon of some sort with him.

There was always a revolver in one of the drawers in his bedroom, but a stout walking stick or a poker would be just as effective if used by someone as strong and athletic as himself.

Then he thought with a smile that he could fight any ordinary intruder with his fists and enjoy doing so.

When he was at Oxford, he had been the University's champion pugilist at his weight and he had given a good account of himself in the ring when he was in the Army.

It struck him that he had not fought for some time and he might even enjoy a fight, as long as there were not too many men to cope with at the same time..

He reasoned that if there had been several, Rufus would have barked rather than just sniffed at the door and growled.

He reached the top of the staircase and in front of him was the door that opened onto the roof and he saw that it was open.

He went out rather cautiously and then he saw standing just ahead of him, looking towards the East, a slim figure in white.

He knew at once who it was and a perception he had had before about Lorena told him why she was there.

It was many years since the Duke had stood on the roof to see the dawn break and he knew now that it was an experience that Lorena would want to enjoy while she was at Mere.

Someone, and he suspected it must have been Mr. Ashley, had told her how beautiful it could be.

Even as the Duke stood looking at her, he knew that the sky was lightening and the brilliance of the stars had begun to fade.

Now he could see Lorena's features, her small straight nose and pointed chin, silhouetted against the sky.

Her head was lifted so that the long line of her neck also was revealed and she looked, he thought, as if she was a statue put there like the marble urns that surmounted the entrance of the house.

He moved forward to stand beside her.

She did not turn her head, but he sensed that she was aware of him and because he knew that she would expect it of him, he stood looking towards the East, as she was doing, without speaking.

The sky lightened further and the first paleness on the horizon deepened to gold, its rays moving up to sweep away the sable of the night and the stars, which only in the West lingered now behind them.

Then, just before the sun itself appeared on the horizon, the Duke felt Lorena's hand slip into his.

He tightened his fingers on hers and felt as he did so that she gave a little quiver, although whether it was excitement because of what she was watching or because he was touching her, he did not know.

Then almost dramatically the sun was there, golden and radiant, at first a vivid streak of flame and then dazzling the eyes with the intensity of its fire.

The Duke knew that Lorena held her breath at the same time holding tightly on to him, so that he felt that they were joined in watching something so splendid and so overwhelmingly beautiful.

The glory in the East intensified and it was day.

Still neither Lorena nor the Duke moved.

Then he felt her hold on his fingers slacken and, because he knew that she was spellbound, he let her go.

She gave a deep sigh that seemed to come from the very depths of her being.

She turned to look at him, her eyes holding the sunshine and her face, he thought, was transfigured with a beauty that he had never witnessed before.

She smiled at him and then without speaking moved away across the roof and disappeared down the staircase that she had come up on.

The Duke stood staring after her as if he could hardly believe that she had left him.

It seemed somehow incredible that they should have gone through such a strange experience together and yet she had nothing to say about it.

But he realised that in leaving him she had done the right thing.

There were no words to describe what they had seen and to talk about it would somehow have spoilt what was too perfect to put into words.

He knew without being told that it was what Lorena had felt and, although it had surprised him, she had been right in behaving as she had. But it was, he thought, exactly what he might have expected of her.

The Duke looked away towards the sun.

It was shining now on the vast acres of his estate and he could see the woods, the meadows, the streams and the farms with their animals spread out before him, almost as if it was a map that could move and live,

'Mine, all mine,' he thought.

Then he knew that it was much more.

It was a sacred trust that had been handed to him by his father and his ancestors before him and one that he in his turn must hand to his son and those who would follow in his footsteps.

*

Lorena slept rather later than usual and when she awoke she felt as if she had experienced something so precious and so perfect that she would hold it forever in her heart.

She knew that what made it more wonderful and more marvellous than it would otherwise have been was the fact that the Duke had shared that magical moment with her.

She did not know how he was aware that she was on the roof. She only accepted it like a small miracle that he should suddenly be beside her and, without even thinking about it, she could hold onto him.

When Mr. Ashley had mentioned that the view from the roof was really stupendous and the finest in the whole County, she had known the moment when she wanted to see it.

Often in Rome she had risen early to go to the window and watch the dawn break over the City, shining as if it was an act of faith particularly on the Dome of St. Peter's.

She reckoned that the view from the Convent would be nothing compared with the view that would be afforded at Mere, which was built on high ground and being so tall commanded the view over a great distance.

She had not been disappointed in what she had expected to see.

She had known it was a moment that she would never forget nor could she forget the feelings that the Duke had evoked when his fingers had tightened on hers.

She was aware too, when she went back in to her bedroom and slipped into bed, that what she felt was love.

It was in fact what she had been feeling for him for a long time, but she had been afraid to give it a name even to herself.

"*I love him!*" she whispered. "And it is exactly what I expected love would be like, spiritual and perfect and like the sun from God."

She wanted to pray in gratitude for the wonder that she was feeling, but it was really a paean of joy because the emotions that rippled through her could not be expressed in any other way.

"I love him! *I love him*!" she repeated over and over again to herself.

For the moment it did not dim her joy to know that he would never love her and that he would never be anything personal or intimate or other than what he had been when she first saw him, a Prince in a Fairy Palace!

'Wherever I go, whatever happens to me,' she thought, 'he will always be there in my mind and nothing can ever take away from me the rapture I felt just now when we watched the dawn together.'

Vaguely and far away, as if in the shadows, her brain told her that he belonged to the Countess, but for the moment even that was of no significance beside what she had felt and what in a way she had received, a blessing that could come only from God.

'To love anyone so wonderful is a privilege and an honour,' Lorena told herself. 'And I can pray for him and feel that perhaps in a very small way my prayers will protect him.'

She could not help feeling that the Countess was the wrong person for anybody so understanding and sympathetic as the Duke.

Then she told herself humbly that she was no judge and she understood that the Countess would fight to keep him. To lose such a man, if he had loved her, would be almost a death blow.

Lorena fell asleep thinking of the Duke and she was sure that while she slept she dreamt of him and, when she awoke much later, it was to feel that in some way he was still with her and her hand was still held in his.

When she went downstairs, having already had her breakfast, which Emily had brought to her room as she had slept so late, she found Sir Hugo and Perry waiting to take her riding.

She longed to ask where the Duke was, but while she was still wondering how to frame the question. Sir Hugo said,

"Most of the party have gone on without us and the Duke is seeing his Agent, so we will not wait for him."

Lorena longed to reply that it was the one thing she wanted to do, but she guessed that her uncle would think it strange.

Instead she mounted the horse that was waiting outside the door and tried to feel that she was so lucky to be riding that it would be shameful to ask for more.

She wanted the Duke to be there and wanted to see him riding his magnificent black stallion as if he was part of the horse and she wanted to see his face and to hear his voice.

They rode for nearly two hours and then, as they turned for home, Lorena felt an inward excitement because in a very short while she would see the Duke again.

~163~

'I love him!' she said to herself. 'But I must be careful. I must never let him guess for one moment what I feel and most of all I must never let anyone else have the slightest suspicion.'

She knew that the one person she feared if she became suspicious was the Countess.

As she thought of how beautiful Daisy Hellingford was, she felt as if a shadow passed across the sun.

*

The Duke was in his library signing some papers that his secretary had brought for him when the Countess came into the room.

She was looking extremely beautiful in a gown of pale mauve chiffon and a large-brimmed hat trimmed with wisteria.

"I am afraid I am busy, Daisy," the Duke said automatically, but his secretary added quickly,

"This is the last one, Your Grace. I must apologise for taking up so much of your time."

There was nothing that the Duke could do in the circumstances and, as the secretary left the room with the signed letters, the Duke rose to his feet to walk to the fireplace where Daisy Hellingford was waiting for him.

"I did not expect you down so early, Daisy," he said. "In fact I intend to go riding now that I have finished my letters. Why do you not come with me?"

The Duke knew as he spoke that it was a quite pointless invitation because Daisy disliked riding and never got on a horse if she could possibly help it.

"I want to talk to you, Alstone."

The Duke resigned himself to what he knew he would have to hear sooner or later.

"Do you want to talk here," he asked, "or shall we go out into the garden?"

"What I have to say should be said at once," Daisy replied, "and where it is said does not matter one way or the other."

"Very well," the Duke agreed.

"You are behaving in a very extraordinary manner, Alstone, and I want an explanation. First, ever since I arrived here there has been something going on between you and your friends that I have not been informed about and secondly you have been avoiding me."

The Duke opened his lips to reply, but before he could speak she held up her hand.

"I have not finished," she went on. "Last week in London you were somewhat evasive. I told myself that it was because we had too many parties to attend and too many people to see, but that here at Mere it would be different."

She paused for breath and the Duke began,

"Now listen to me, Daisy – "

"You listen to *me*!" she flashed. "I love you, Alstone. And I believed that you loved me, but you

~165~

have not been near me since I arrived here. I want to know the reason why."

It was, the Duke knew, the crux of the whole problem.

He had told himself already that he had to accept it sooner or later and, as Daisy was intent on a showdown, there was nothing he could do but have it now.

He walked away from the hearthrug towards the window, wondering as he did so why women must always give voice to what is quite obvious without the need for words.

He stood looking out at the sunshine and then said,

"I think, Daisy, we are both adult enough to accept things that happen to us in our lives without recriminations and without having to spell them out in words of two syllables."

There was no reply from Daisy for a moment and he turned curiously to see an expression on her face that he supposed he might have anticipated.

It was one of astonishment.

"Are you saying that you are tired of me?" she asked after a while in a strangled voice.

Even as she spoke, there was a note in her voice that told the Duke that to her such a development was completely and utterly inconceivable.

"I am not exactly tired," the Duke said evasively, "but I think, Daisy, we are both aware that our *affaire de coeur* has not quite the spontaneity and perhaps the excitement it had when it first started."

"That is a lie as far as I am concerned," Daisy snapped. "I love you, Alstone, and *my* feelings have not changed."

"I don't think that is quite true. At the same time I am not prepared to argue about it. When we return to London, I will send you a present, which I hope you will always keep as a memento of the great happiness that we have enjoyed with each other and I hope we shall always remain friends."

As he spoke, he thought that it sounded priggish, but he could not imagine how else he could finish with Daisy.

Certainly, as far as he was concerned, everything was over and she had to accept it whether she wished to or not.

"Are you really brushing me off in this manner?" Daisy asked. "I have never been so insulted, never in the whole of my life! I can assure you, Alstone, that you are making a very grave mistake and it is something you will deeply regret."

There was no doubt that she intended to make him regret it, but for the moment the Duke could only bow before the storm and there was no chance for him to say anything.

He had always been told that Daisy Hellingford had a temper, but while she was happy exerting her power over him and, because he in many ways had found her fascinating, he had never seen her in a rage until now.

As he watched her working herself up into a flaming passion and heard the vitriolic reproach that dropped from her lips, he knew that the one thing he really disliked was a woman who lost control of herself.

He supposed it might have been expected from anyone like Daisy as, if she was fiery in one way, she would be fiery in another.

He felt, however, that she not only degraded herself in losing her temper but also degraded him.

He wanted to stop her and prevent the scene between them from becoming uglier as it was doing minute by minute, but it would have been easier to halt a cyclone or calm a tempest at sea.

Daisy raged on and on and the Duke found himself disliking her more with every second that passed.

*

Lorena walked in through the front door, followed by Sir Hugo and Perry.

"We have plenty of time to change before luncheon," Sir Hugo declared as he glanced at the huge crystal and gilt French clock that stood in a corner of the hall.

"Thank goodness for that," Perry remarked before Lorena could answer. "I want to have a bath. I have never known it to be as hot as it is today."

"It must certainly be nearly in the eighties," Sir Hugo said.

As all three moved towards the staircase, Lord Carnforth came from a salon and walked towards them.

"Have you had a good ride?" he asked.

"Delightful," Sir Hugo replied. "I thought you were going to join us."

"I was waiting for Alstone," Lord Carnforth said, "but I waited in vain."

He dropped his voice so that the servants would not hear and added,

"Daisy is making a scene in the library and I should think that the temperature at luncheon will be well below zero!"

"What has upset her?" Perry asked quickly.

"I have no idea, I only know that I have missed my ride!"

Lorena went up the stairs in silence.

She wondered what the Countess could be making a scene about now and she hoped, with a little tremor of fear, that she had not in some mysterious way found out that she and the Duke had been on the roof together at dawn.

She felt sure that it was impossible and yet one never knew.

~169~

She wished, because she was frightened, that she did not have to go down to luncheon, but, even if she did not do so, she would have to meet the Countess sooner or later and, if she was angry, she was sure that no one could prevent her from saying so.

She wondered if she could confide in her uncle and tell him that, although she had not meant to be alone with the Duke again, it had just happened because he had joined her.

Then she knew that she could not bear to speak of that moment of happiness to anyone. It would spoil it.

It would spoil a perfect moment that she had placed in a shrine within herself so that it could be kept sacred from the world. Especially the world that contained the Duke's friends.

'Please, God – please don't let her – find out – where we were,' she prayed.

She went on saying the same prayer all the time she was changing her clothes.

She went down to luncheon apprehensively to find that most of the house party, who had gathered in the Blue Drawing Room, had their heads together and were talking in low voices, which meant that they were discussing their host and the Countess.

The Marchioness of Trumpington put out her hand to Lorena as she walked in and drew her away from the others to move near a window.

"Come and talk to me, Lorena," she suggested. "I want you to tell me about your life at home when your father and mother were alive."

"I would like to do so," Lorena said simply, "but I am afraid you might find it rather dull. We lived in a small Vicarage in a very quiet part of the country, but we were very happy."

"It does not matter whether your house is big or small, if you are happy," the Marchioness said with a smile.

"That is what I realised when I was in Rome. The girls used to talk about their stately homes, their Castles and one or two even lived in Palaces. But I knew that, however grand and important they were, I would give anything in the world merely to go home to my father and mother so that we could be together again."

"That was what was important?" the Marchioness asked.

"It was important because we were a family," Lorena explained. "Papa used to say to me that families were especially blessed because Jesus had chosen to have a father and mother and quite an ordinary home until He started to preach."

"But supposing," the Marchioness said, "there had been no love in your home?"

"It is impossible to imagine that," Lorena answered, "because Mama loved Papa so deeply and they loved me."

~171~

She paused for a moment and then carried on,

"Mama once said that it was the woman who makes a home and who gives it the love that encircles it with happiness."

"Your mother loved your father, so it was easy for her," the Marchioness murmured.

"Mama gave everybody love. The people in the village adored her and her friends all came to her when they were in trouble because she would help them. She said to me once, 'we may be poor, Lorena, but love is without price. It is more valuable than any other commodity in the whole world'."

The Marchioness smiled at her.

"Thank you, dear child."

As she spoke, she rose to her feet.

Lorena had been so intent on what she was saying that she had not noticed that the Duke had joined the party and the butler had announced luncheon.

Only as they went towards the dining room did she realise with a sense of relief that the Countess of Hellingford was not present and there was another lady sitting beside the Duke at the head of the table.

She felt shy of looking at him because she was so vividly aware of his presence and she did not meet his eyes until halfway through luncheon.

Then, as if she could not help herself, she found herself gazing at him and in that second his eyes held hers.

She felt that they spoke without words and that they were both thinking of what had happened at dawn.

Then, as the Marchioness spoke to him, he turned his head and, as if she came back from a long way away, Lorena realised that the man sitting next to her was waiting for her to reply to something he had said.

After what seemed a very drawn-out meal, the whole party moved automatically into the Blue Drawing Room.

"As we have not made any plans for this afternoon," the Duke said, "I wondered if you would think it amusing to drive or ride over to the Folly. It is about five miles away and was built by one of my ancestors who had too much money and too little sense. We could have a picnic tea there."

"That sounds delightful," the Marchioness exclaimed.

"I am prepared to look at all the Follies, wherever they are built, providing I can race you on one of your horses, Alstone," Lord Carnforth proposed.

"That is what I would, like too," Major Fane agreed.

"We might have a Steeplechase," someone else said. "I am sure that Alstone could provide us with some enviable prizes."

"It is certainly an idea," the Duke said. "What about you, Perry?"

"I am prepared to race anyone and everyone," Perry replied, "as long as I can choose my horse."

"You can have any one in the stable as long as you don't choose mine," the Duke chuckled.

"That is taking an unfair advantage!" one man called out.

"Not really," the Duke replied, "because if I win, I promise not to take the first prize, but to pass it on to whoever is second."

"Are we going to draw up some rules about this race, Alstone?" Archie Carnforth asked. "I think most of us know this part of the country anyway and personally I think it would be more fun if it was a Point-to-Point from here to the Folly."

"You must let us go first," the Marchioness said, "because otherwise we will not be there in time to greet the victor."

"That is sensible," the Duke approved. "Now who is going by carriage and who is going to ride?"

He looked towards Lorena as he spoke and he knew by the light in her eyes that she wanted to ride.

"The ladies can ride if they wish," he said, "but they may not compete."

"Are you suggesting," asked the Viscountess Storr, "that we are not capable of riding as well as the men?"

"You will certainly look far more attractive when you start," the Duke replied, "but, as this is quite a hard ride, I dread to think of how you will appear by the end of it!"

"Don't be tiresome, Sarah," the Marchioness exclaimed. "I intend to ride and we will leave half-an-hour before those who are going to race, so we will get there in comfort. It is far too hot to be energetic."

"I personally am going to drive," one of the ladies said positively and two of the others agreed that it was their preference as well.

"Well, perhaps we ought to go and get ready," the Marchioness said. "Come along, Lorena, We can only hope we will not find that all the best horses have been taken before we come down again."

The Marchioness was already moving towards the door when the Countess of Hellingford appeared.

She had changed her gown and was wearing, to Lorena's surprise, a flat motoring hat from which streamed a long chiffon veil.

Over one arm she carried a dustcoat such as ladies always wore when they were in an open car and both her hands were beneath it as if it were a muff.

She swept imperiously down the room, stopped just before she reached Lorena and the Marchioness and stood staring at the Duke, who detached himself from the men he was talking to.

"I have now come to say 'goodbye', Alstone," the Countess said loudly, "to you and to your friends."

Everybody stopped talking and there was silence as she went on,

"You have made it very clear that you do *not* wish to have me here and I certainly have no desire to stay where I am not wanted."

She paused for a moment and the Duke interposed,

"Please, Daisy – "

The Countess continued as if he had not spoken,

"I am going back to London and I shall never, make no mistake, *never* set foot in this accursed place again! I loathe Mere and I loathe you, Alstone, for what you have done to me!"

She paused again.

Then she went on distinctly and with a venomous note in her voice that was unmistakable,

"But make no mistake – if you will not make *me* happy, no other woman shall have what belongs to me!"

Before she said the last three words she had drawn her right hand from beneath the dustcoat and Lorena saw with horror that she held a small revolver in her hand.

The Countess spoke the words '*belongs to me*' slowly, accentuating them as if she wished them to be particularly dramatic.

Then she pointed the pistol so that the bullet would hit the Duke below the waist.

But before she could pull the trigger, Lorena, driven by instinct that was swifter than thought, seized the Countess's arm and forced it upwards.

There was a resounding explosion as the bullet passed just above the Duke's shoulder, grazing the cloth of his coat to bury itself in the mirror over the mantelpiece and smash the glass into a thousand pieces.

There was a scream, but otherwise everyone else present was astounded into silence.

Then, as Lorena released her grip, the Countess brought down the revolver with all her strength on the girl who had prevented her revenge from being effective.

It caught Lorena on the side of the temple and she fell to the ground as if poleaxed.

Then, as Perry snatched the revolver from Daisy's hand, the Duke moved forward to kneel beside Lorena.

Lorena was unconscious and was therefore quite unaware of the pandemonium that then broke out.

Everybody was talking and exclaiming at once, while the Countess, her eyes flashing and a flush on her cheeks, merely stood staring at the Duke, who did not even raise his head to look at her.

"How could you do such a terrible thing?" Sir Hugo demanded angrily. "You might have killed Alstone and you would have hanged for it!"

"It would not have killed him. I would merely have stopped his philandering, if your niece had not interfered."

"You should be very grateful that she did," Sir Hugo retorted. "Think of the scandal it would have caused if you had killed or injured Alstone. If anyone talks about what has happened here, the Press will get hold of it and that would be disastrous."

The rest of the members of the house party were all standing and staring at Daisy as if they could not believe what they had just seen.

The Duke, with Lorena in his arms, rose to his feet.

"Send for a doctor," he said sharply to Perry, who happened to be standing closest to him.

Without saying another word he walked towards the door.

As he disappeared, a hubbub of voices broke out and Sir Hugo held up his hand.

"Now listen to me, all of you," he demanded. "I want you to swear by everything you hold sacred that not one of you will mention what has just occurred here to anyone outside this room."

The Countess made a derisive sound and made as if to leave, but Sir Hugo barred her way.

"You will swear too, Daisy," he ordered her, "and make no mistake, I am not trying to save your reputation but my niece's."

"Your niece is not involved except that she prevented me from treating Alstone as he deserves!" Daisy snapped.

"You know as well as I do that, if it was known that she saved Alstone's life and that she was involved in a quarrel that concerned you and him, the child would be snubbed socially in a manner that would be most unfair and would do her a great deal of harm."

He saw that the Countess was undecided and so he went on,

"If you do *not* agree to what I suggest, then I shall not only have no compunction in telling your husband the truth of this whole unsavoury affair but I shall also make it my business to acquaint Their Majesties with the facts of the matter!"

The Countess looked at him in surprise.

Then, as she realised that she had been defeated, she shrugged her shoulders.

"Very well then," she mumbled, "I give you my promise, but I don't see why Alstone should get away scot-free."

Sir Hugo did not reply, he merely looked at the other members of the house party and asked,

"Will you all give me your solemn promise without reservation that nothing will be said about Daisy's behaviour or the very fortunate way that Lorena saved our host from being killed or wounded?"

"I promise!"

Everybody in the party then murmured the words simultaneously and Sir Hugo said,

"Thank you. And now, Daisy, I suggest the sooner you go the better."

"I have every intention of leaving," the Countess replied with what dignity she could muster. "But I would like to speak to Alstone first."

"That is something I have no intention of allowing you to do," Sir Hugo intervened. "You have done enough damage for one day. Go back to London, Daisy, and thank your lucky stars that it is not a great deal worse than it is. You are a wicked woman and I hope I do not meet you again for a very long time."

The Countess tossed her head imperiously and walked from the room.

Sir Hugo watched her go and then drew a large white handkerchief from his breast pocket and wiped his forehead.

"All I can say is thank God for Lorena," Perry remarked. "Now I must call for the doctor, as Alstone told me to do."

"And I will go and see how she is," Sir Hugo then proposed.

They left the room together and the others who were left behind all began to talk at once.

Sir Hugo could hear their voices as he hurried up the stairs.

He found that the Duke had already laid Lorena down on her bed.

Her face was very pale and she looked young, frail and vulnerable and there was already a large angry red mark on the side of her temple where the revolver had struck her.

The Duke was standing by the bed and looking down at her as Sir Hugo came to his side.

"I have not rung for the maid at the moment," the Duke said, "because I thought we first ought to decide what we should say both to the servants and, of course, to the doctor."

"I have made everyone in the house party swear that what has happened shall go no further," Sir Hugo informed him in a low voice.

"I thought you would. Thank you, Hugo."

"I was thinking of Lorena and I threatened Daisy that I will not only tell her husband but also the King and Queen if she breathes a word of what actually occurred here."

"She must be out of her mind," the Duke said in a low voice.

"I warned you a long time ago that she is uncontrolled and rotten to the core."

"You were right," the Duke nodded briefly.

Sir Hugo looked at Lorena.

"I think we should just say that the child slipped on the polished parquet and fell against one of the tables. It could have happened that way."

"I suppose so," the Duke agreed. "I will see that the servants hear that story and you can tell the doctor too."

He moved towards the door and Sir Hugo said,

"If I was you, Alstone, I should leave the others to get over the shock. They were chattering like an aviary of parrots when I came up the stairs."

"I have every intention of going somewhere *alone*," the Duke said, accentuating the word.

"I think that is wise of you," Sir Hugo remarked and put out his hand towards the bell-pull.

CHAPTER SEVEN

Kelvin Fane walked into the library where the Duke was at his desk writing.

"I am leaving now, Alstone."

The Duke looked up in surprise.

"So early, Kelvin? I was not expecting you to go until later."

"I want to get to London early this afternoon," Major Fane replied, "because I have made a decision that I think you will approve of."

"What is that?" the Duke asked.

He rose from his desk and walked across the room to stand with his back to the fireplace.

"I have been thinking," Kelvin. Fane said, as if he was choosing his words with care, "that there seems a strong likelihood that we shall be at war with Germany before we are very much older."

"You really think it possibility?" the Duke enquired.

Kelvin Fane nodded.

"I was talking to the Commander-in-Chief last month and he is convinced that we should be prepared, which we are certainly not at the moment."

"In which case, what do you intend to do about it?" the Duke asked.

"I am going to the War Office as soon as I arrive in London to apply to be posted to the Staff College at Camberley for a course."

The Duke looked surprised and Kelvin Fane added,

"It is what the Commander-in-Chief suggested to me. He was really rather flattering and he told me,

'You are one of the men, Fane, who, if there is a war, I would like to have on my staff'."

The Major paused for a moment before he added,

"I laughed at the time, but now I have come to the conclusion that it is time I did something a little more serious than waste my intelligence with women like Sarah."

This was such plain speaking that the Duke was astounded.

He had never known Kelvin Fane to talk to him so frankly before on matters that were intimate and private.

He was silent for a moment and then he said,

"Has this sudden decision on your part anything to do with what occurred on Monday?"

"Of course it has," Kelvin Fane replied. "But, even before Daisy behaved in such an outrageous manner, it was Lorena actually who made me realise that I was wasting my life."

The Duke raised his eyebrows as he asked,

"Is your interest in Lorena serious?"

"Shall I say that I am thinking about her seriously and I intend to see her as soon as she leaves here. After that I may be able to answer you more positively."

When he had finished speaking, he held out his hand,

"Goodbye, Alstone, and thank you for a very unusual visit to Mere. I cannot think of any other way to describe it."

The Duke took his hand and suggested,

"I will come and see you off."

"No, stay where you are," Kelvin Fane replied. "I can see that you are busy."

"I am writing a speech that I want to make in the House of Lords. It has been on my conscience for some time, but I have been too lazy to set it down in writing."

"We all seem to have been activated out of our indolence these last few days," Kelvin Fane remarked.

He walked towards the door and, as he reached it, he turned back to say,

"I have paid my debt to Hugo. I consider that he won the contest hands down. And by the way, Lionel Dartford is waiting to see you. Shall I send him in?"

"Yes, of course," the Duke nodded.

When he was alone, he did not go back to his writing desk. Instead he stood looking across the great library with a very thoughtful expression in his eyes.

Only a few minutes passed before the door opened and Lord Dartford came into the room.

"Like Fane I only want to say 'goodbye'," he began, "and, of course, to thank you for your hospitality."

"I wanted to see you anyway," the Duke replied, "but everybody is leaving earlier than I expected."

Lord Dartford grinned.

"I think the truth is that they are feeling a little embarrassed."

"Which is not surprising," the Duke concurred drily.

Lord Dartford held out his hand.

"Well, goodbye, then."

"No, wait a minute," the Duke said. "I have something to suggest to you which I think you might find interesting."

"What is that?"

"I had a letter a week ago from the Maharajah of Cochapour. He asked me if I could recommend anybody completely honest and trustworthy in this country who could buy him a large number of polo ponies for his team."

"One of the best in India," Lord Dartford murmured.

"And who would also purchase on his behalf," the Duke continued, "a great quantity of furnishings, which he needs for a new Palace he is building."

The Duke smiled as he continued,

"You can imagine what they will be, very expensive chandeliers, gold-framed mirrors and naturally superlative carpets, all of which will be extremely costly."

Lord Dartford was listening to the Duke with rapt attention, but he did not say anything and the Duke went on,

"The Maharajah, who, as you are aware, is one of the richest men in India suggested that whoever undertakes to serve him in this way would be entitled not only to a salary and expenses but also to a large commission on everything that is purchased."

The Duke paused before he added,

"I can think of no one more qualified to fill the position than you, Lionel."

Lord Dartford drew in a deep breath,

"Do you really mean that, Alstone? It is something I would very much enjoy doing, besides the fact that I have made such a fool of myself not only over the money I have lost here but in buying a number of dud shares. Actually I am in 'Queer Street'."

"Then this will get you out of it," the Duke said. "As it happens, I had anticipated that you would accept my suggestion and I have already written to the Maharajah and put forward your name. I told him that I would trust your judgement on horseflesh anywhere and that in furnishing his Palace your taste would be as good as mine!"

Lord Dartford made an inarticulate little sound and the Duke went on quickly,

"Before you leave, look in my secretary's office and read the letter in case there are any amendments you would like to make."

"I don't know how to thank you – " Lord Dartford started in a hoarse voice.

"I shall be very embarrassed if you try," the Duke said. "I think really we should be thanking Lorena. It was she who brought to my notice the fact that the stakes played in this house were far too high. This is something that will not happen in the future."

"She is the pluckiest girl I have ever known in my whole life!" Lord Dartford exclaimed. "Will you tell her so when she is better? Also tell Hugo, if I don't see him, that he has been proved right so indisputably over the *Pygmalion* contest that Archie will have to pay up and like it!"

"He certainly will," the Duke agreed, "and I will see that he does."

There were more expressions of gratitude on Lord Dartford's part before the two men parted.

The Duke returned to his desk and had been writing for some time when the Marchioness of Trumpington, looking extremely attractive in a motoring hat with clouds of blue chiffon trailing from it, peeped round the door.

"Are you alone, Alstone?" she enquired.

"Enid!" the Duke exclaimed. "I had no idea that it was so late. I knew that you and Jack were leaving at three o'clock and I meant to be waiting for you."

"It's not yet three and Jack is fussing about the car," the Marchioness replied, "but I want to speak to you."

"Of course. Come and sit down."

The Marchioness seated herself on the sofa, looked up at the Duke and smiled.

"I can see that you are apprehensive," she said, "but you will be pleased at what I have to tell you."

"I do hope so."

"I think you may have anticipated that I might say that Jack and I were going to do something desperate like running away together," the Marchioness stated.

"It had crossed my mind," the Duke admitted. "Something that Jack said the first night you were here made me wonder what I could do to stop you."

"There is no need for you to do anything," the Marchioness answered. "What I have come to tell you, Alstone, is that we had intended to leave England, Jack and I. In fact we came to Mere because we thought that it would be a good opportunity to be together and finalise our plans."

"Now you have changed your minds?" the Duke asked with a note of relief in his voice.

"It was Lorena who did that."

"Lorena?" the Duke exclaimed incredulously.

"She is so young and innocent and yet she has a kind of aura about her which I can only describe as one of goodness."

The Marchioness gave a little sigh.

"It made me remember what I was like at her age, idealistic and romantic, believing that the world was a wonderful place and that if I was happy I would make everybody else happy too."

The Marchioness paused.

The Duke did not speak and after a moment she went on,

"When I looked at her and listened to her, I knew that what Jack and I contemplated would not only hurt my husband, who in his own way has shown me nothing but kindness, but would also damage a great number of other people, simply because they are our friends."

She looked round the library as if she was seeing it for the first time and then she continued,

"Mere and other houses like it, people like yourself, Alstone, and, of course, the Trumpington family in the public's mind stand not only for the grandeur of this country but for its stability."

Her voice deepened as she carried on,

"I have begun to understand that the obligations I owe to my position in the Social world are in a way more important than the dictates of my heart and that also applies to Jack."

The Marchioness made a very expressive little gesture with her hands before she added,

"I love him. I love him desperately and he loves me, but he has a position of great standing in his own County, the people he employs on his estate respect him and his children love him and he loves them."

Her voice trembled for a moment and then she added,

"We will go on seeing each other discreetly and perhaps one day, who knows, Fate may be kind to us.

Until then we will play the parts we have to play and I hope we do so with dignity."

The Duke sat down beside the Marchioness and took her hand in his.

"Thank you for telling me this, Enid. I admire both you and Jack for coming to such a decision, which I know is the right one."

"I am sure it is," the Marchioness replied. "And please tell that sweet child that, as soon as she is well enough, I want her to come and stay with me. If Kitty will not chaperone her, I will do so myself and it is something I would greatly enjoy."

"I will tell Lorena."

"And thank you, Alstone dear," the Marchioness said, "for being the most wonderful friend that Jack and I ever had. I know that, if anyone will help us in the years that lie ahead, it will be you."

"You may be sure of that," the Duke replied.

He kissed the Marchioness's hand and, when they both rose to their feet, she bent forward and kissed him on the cheek.

"Thank you, Alstone," she repeated and there were tears in her eyes.

The Duke walked with her to the hall, found that Lord Gilmour was waiting beside the motor car at the front door and saw them off on their journey to London.

He thought as he walked back up the steps into the house that he might have felt very differently had they been driving in the opposite direction and setting off for the Continent.

The Marchioness was right, their positions carried responsibilities that neither of them could ignore.

The Duke was walking across the hall when Sir Hugo came down the staircase.

"Has Enid gone?" he asked. "I wanted to say 'goodbye' to her."

"She has just left."

"Well, I shall see them in London."

"Yes, in London."

Sir Hugo reached the hall and the Duke asked,

"How is Lorena? Has the doctor seen her?"

"Yes, he was here about an hour ago," Sir Hugo replied. "She will be able to get up tomorrow. He does not wish her to travel until Thursday, if that is all right with you."

"Of course it is and I would rather like to talk to her now if that is possible."

"I have just moved her into the boudoir next to her bedroom," Sir Hugo replied, "she is to have tea there."

"Then I will go and talk to her," the Duke said, "I have various messages to give her from the guests who have already left and Enid has suggested that she should go and stay with her if Kitty does not want her."

As he spoke, he glanced at Sir Hugo and saw his lips tighten in a hard line.

"Have you and Kitty made any decision about Lorena's future?" he asked.

"In this instance it will be a question of what *I* want," Sir Hugo replied.

The Duke's eyes twinkled, but he did not say anything.

Sir Hugo, as if he was anxious to change the subject, then said,

"By the way you will be amused to hear that Archie paid up like a sportsman before he left this morning. He said that he could hardly argue with someone who had made a Grand Slam."

Sir Hugo gave a little laugh.

"What was more, Archie had no wish to argue, because he was in such a hurry to get to London.

"I would not mind betting that his real reason is that he wants to get to the Club before Kelvin or Jack to expound *his* contention that different kinds of water affect the running of a horse!"

The Duke laughed.

"I am sure that Archie will take all the credit for that idea even though we all know it was Lorena's."

"She has certainly done me proud," Sir Hugo smiled. "I don't mind telling you now that, as I waited at Victoria Station, I was very nervous as to what she would be like. But she not only turned up trumps, but, as Archie put it, she made a Grand Slam as well!"

"Will it be all right if I go up to see her now?" the Duke asked.

Sir Hugo had the idea that his host had not been listening to what he had been saying, so he merely replied,

"Yes, of course. She has a nasty bruise on her temple, but otherwise, I don't think there is much wrong."

He realised, however, that he was talking to thin air for the Duke had left and was already climbing the stairs.

*

Lorena, sitting on the *chaise longue* in the boudoir that was attached to her bedroom, was wondering which of the books that Mrs. Kingston had put beside her would be the most intriguing to read.

Her uncle had already told her that they could leave for London on Thursday and she felt almost childishly that, when there was so much at Mere she had to leave behind, it would add to her feeling of regret if she left a half-finished novel as well.

Lying back against the silk cushions with a lace and satin cover over her legs, she looked round the room as if it was another item to store in her memory.

The cupids in the Boucher paintings on the walls echoed those painted on the ceiling, the exquisite pieces of French furniture and the turquoise blue of the curtains and coverings on the Louis XIV chairs were all photographed in her mind permanently.

'Everything at Mere is so lovely,' she told herself.

However, because she must leave it, there was a pain in her breast far more intense than the ache in her temple.

Yet if she was honest, it was the owner of Mere who would haunt her for the rest of her life and would be not only in her mind but in her heart and soul for all Eternity.

'I saved him,' she had mused with an irrepressible elation when she had recovered consciousness.

Although her head had ached almost unbearably and she felt a little sick and shaken by what had occurred, nothing mattered except that the Duke was uninjured and she had been able to prevent the Countess from destroying him as she had tried to do.

'How could any woman be so – cruel – so wicked?' Lorena asked herself.

She knew that because she loved the Duke she wanted to protect him not only from anything that would hurt him spiritually but also from unhappiness and disillusionment.

If he loved the Countess, it would have been terrible for him to watch her behaving in such a manner, but if, as it appeared from what she had said, he no longer loved her, then surely there must have been the humiliation of knowing that he had wasted his love on someone who could behave in such an unrestrained and vulgar way.

'I saved him – then,' Lorena thought, "but – suppose she tries – again?'

It was an inexpressible agony to think that the Duke might again be in danger and that she would not be there to protect him.

Then she told herself that she was being ridiculous.

She could never mean anything in the Duke's life. She had been extremely fortunate in being able to express her love in a way that she had never dreamt of.

It was just chance that she had been in that particular place at that particular moment.

Had she been standing anywhere else in the room, however strong her instinct of danger might have been, she would have been too late to deflect the bullet from where it was intended.

"You were very brave and I am very proud of you," Sir Hugo had said when he came to see her last night after the doctor had departed.

Lorena had longed to ask him what the Duke had said and what he had thought, but she had been too shy and had found it difficult to say anything.

Because Sir Hugo had thought that she was sleepy and should be left to rest as quietly as possible, he had gone away and she had been alone with her thoughts.

Now she knew that, if she opened one of the books that lay at her side, she would find it difficult to concentrate on the pages.

All she would see would be the Duke's face.

As this made her happy and was far more enthralling than anything she could read, she lay back and started to think over all that had happened from the first moment she had met him.

There was that morning when they had gone riding together and then had breakfast alone in the ancient farmhouse.

'That is what I want to do again,' Lorena thought.

But she was asking for the impossible and once she left Mere the Duke would be as inaccessible as the moon.

She closed her eyes as if it would minimise the pain that she knew she would feel when they said 'goodbye'.

Then there was a knock on the door and, before she could answer it, the Duke came into the room.

For a moment, because she was thinking of him so intensely, she could hardly realise that he was actually there and not a part of her imagination.

But, as he walked towards the *chaise longue* where she was lying, she felt the blood rising in her cheeks because of the look in his eyes and because her hair was falling over her shoulders and she was wearing only her dressing gown under the satin and lace cover.

It was a very demure garment that she had worn at the Convent of white crepe, plainly cut and buttoned down the front with a flat collar at the neck and long sleeves.

It made Lorena look, especially with her hair down, very young and at the same time almost ethereal, as if she was not human but one of the classical statues that the Duke had thought her to be when he had seen her standing in the darkness on the roof.

He reached the *chaise longue* and held out his hand.

"How are you, Lorena?" he asked.

"Your uncle said you were well enough to see me."

"I am – quite well," Lorena replied in a voice that did not sound like her own. "Tomorrow I can – get up."

Because he was expecting it, she put out her hand and he held it in both of his.

Then to her surprise he sat down beside her on the edge of the *chaise longue,* rather than in a chair, as she would have expected.

"You are very lovely," he murmured, "and I have often thought that your hair would look as it does now."

Lorena's cheeks were crimson and her eyes flickered and, as she looked down, her eyelashes were dark against her skin.

He still kept her hand in his and after a moment he said,

"I must start, before we say all the things we have to tell each other, by thanking you for saving my life."

He felt her fingers quiver and knew that it was because she was afraid of what might have happened to him.

Then he went on,

"I want you to try to forget what happened. It was ugly and unpleasant and it is not the sort of thing I want you ever to think about again."

"I-I was – afraid for – you."

"I know," the Duke replied, "and it was very perceptive and clever of you to have anticipated what might happen. But I am safe, so please don't think about it anymore."

There was a note of authority in his voice and Lorena replied,

"I will – try."

"There are a great number of other things to think about," the Duke smiled, "but first of all I have a message for you from the Marchioness. She would like you to go and stay with her not only on a visit but, if you wish, indefinitely."

Lorena looked at him in surprise.

"You mean – I could live – with her?"

"That, I think, is what she would like, but I believe your uncle has other ideas."

"Uncle Hugo did say – something that made me think that he – might want me – but I have a feeling that Aunt Kitty will – send me away."

"At least you have two propositions to consider," the Duke remarked, "and I have a third."

Lorena looked at him but did not speak and he thought that it would be impossible for any other woman's eyes to be more revealing.

He looked down at the hand he still held in his and then said as if he was choosing his words carefully,

"I expect you will remember, because you are well-read, that the Greeks always said that, if you saved a man's life, he was your responsibility forever."

There was silence and Lorena's fingers were tense as the Duke continued quietly,

"I am wondering therefore, Lorena, what you intend to do about me."

"I-I don't – understand."

"I think you should look after me," he said, "for I need you as I have never needed anyone else."

He knew by the way her fingers quivered that a vague understanding of what he was saying had come to her mind.

At the same time she dared not believe it.

"What – are you, asking me to – do?" she enquired in a voice he could barely hear.

"I am asking you to marry me, my darling," the Duke said. "I knew that I loved you when we watched the dawn together, but I have had no chance of telling you so until now."

"Y-you – love – me?"

The words held a joy that was almost untranslatable into sound.

"I love you!" the Duke continued. "And I think, perhaps because already our minds are so close to each other, that you love me a little."

"I love you! *Of course* I love you!" Lorena sighed. "I love you until it is a glory that fills the whole sky – but I cannot – marry – you."

The words were almost inaudible, but the Duke heard them.

"Did you say you would not marry me?" he asked incredulously.

It had never occurred to him that a woman, any woman, would refuse him if he offered her marriage and least of all Lorena.

"I cannot – marry you," Lorena said and now her voice was firm, "but I shall always be – inexpressibly proud that you – asked me."

The Duke's fingers tightened on hers.

"Why will you not marry me?" he asked. "You said you love me."

"I do love you and it is the most – wonderful thing imaginable that – you should love me too – but I am not the right wife for you – as I would not be able to make you – happy."

"You are thinking of me?" the Duke asked.

"Of course I am – thinking of – you."

There was a faint smile on the Duke's lips as she went on,

"When I knew I – loved you – I never dreamt – never imagined for one second that you would ever – love me – and, although it is such an – agony to think of leaving you – "

Her voice broke on the words, but then she went on,

"I know my memories of you will – always be in my heart – and will help me when I can no longer – see you and no longer – hear your voice."

"You feel like that and yet you will not marry me?"

"It is – because I love you – so much."

Her voice trembled as she continued,

"I was thinking just now before you came into the room that – because I love you I want to – protect you and to take care of you and prevent anyone else from – injuring you not only physically, but by hurting your – mind or your feelings."

She drew a deep breath before she said,

"That is what I should want to do – if I – married you."

"But you are refusing me?"

"Because I could not take – part in your life – or be – accepted by your friends."

She looked straight up at him, wanting him to understand.

"I am not only – ignorant – but foolish where they are – concerned – and – "

She stopped.

"And?" the Duke prompted.

Lorena did not speak and he asked very gently,

"Tell me what else you feel."

She glanced up at him and her words came with a rush,

"I am – shocked at the way they – behave!"

Now it was impossible for her to look at the Duke and, because she thought that he would be angry, she held on to his hand tightly as she had held it before when they had watched the dawn.

The Duke understood everything that she was trying to say and the expression on his face was one that no woman had ever seen before.

"So to save me from being unhappy," he said, "you are prepared to go away and leave me, knowing that our love for each other is something so unique and so overwhelming that to me it is like the sun we saw filling the sky with its fire and beauty."

"Is it – really like – that to you?" Lorena whispered.

"All that and very much more," the Duke replied. "And, as you and I saw the sun sweep away the night, so our love will sweep from our lives all that is dark and ugly and everything, my darling, that shocks you."

"Supposing – just supposing you become – unhappy because you – married me?"

"If you will not marry me, I shall be so abjectly miserable that I shall think that life is not worth living."

She made a little sound of joy and the Duke went on,

"But if you are worried, my darling one, about not being accepted by my friends, I have something to tell you."

"What is – that?" Lorena asked him.

"The reason why your uncle brought you to Mere," the Duke said, "was that he and Lord Carnforth had an argument over a play called *Pygmalion*. Have you read it?"

"Yes, I read it while I was here," Lorena answered. "I found the book in your library."

"I intend to read it myself, but I have not yet had time," the Duke said. "But you, having read it, will understand that the argument arose because Lord Carnforth said that what the Professor had done in transforming a girl, I think her name was Eliza Doolittle, so that she was accepted in Society was completely impossible."

Lorena's eyes were wide with interest as he went on,

"Your uncle, on the other hand, claimed that it was perfectly credible. There was a wordy duel between the two with all the men present taking sides. Then Lord Carnforth demanded that your uncle should prove his point by bringing a young girl to Mere who would be accepted at the end of her visit as one of the Windlemere Set."

"And that, was – me?" Lorena asked in amazement.

"Your uncle had no idea of what you would be like," the Duke replied, "but, because he and Archie Carnforth are often at loggerheads with each other, he agreed to the competition."

"That first night," Lorena murmured, "when everybody looked at me in a – curious manner, I had a feeling that there was something I did not – understand."

"You indeed charmed us all, Lorena, and, when we had breakfast together the next morning, when I knew that you were not in the least what I expected, in fact I felt nervous because you intrigued me so much."

"Nervous?" Lorena questioned.

"Shall I say you enchanted me? I just knew that I was falling in love."

His face drew a little nearer to hers as he carried on,

"I felt as I had never felt before not only a desire to touch you and kiss you because you were so lovely, but I also wanted to protect you, to look after you and keep you safe from anything that might harm you."

"That – is what I – felt about you!"

"I think love, real love, arouses everybody in the same way," the Duke said.

He bent nearer still as he declared very softly,

"How can I deny what is the most wonderful thing in the world, a love that tells me that you are the woman I have been looking for all my life?"

"And you are the – Prince Charming I have – dreamt about for years."

Lorena was not able to say any more for the Duke's lips were on hers and his arms were around her.

He held her very close and thought that no other woman could be more soft, more sweet and more pure and good.

Then, as he felt an almost incredible rapture rise within him, which was very different from anything he had ever known before, he knew, as Lorena did, that it was an ecstasy that came from God.

What she felt for the Duke was like the sun sweeping over the horizon, blinding and glorious, its rays shooting up into the sky so that the stars faded before its glory.

She felt as if the Duke took her heart and soul from between her lips and made them his and she thought too that the strength of his arms gave her a security that she had not felt since her father and mother had died.

But now she was his and never again would she feel lonely and afraid.

The Duke raised his head to look down at her and, because she was so happy, her eyes were full of sunshine as she murmured,

"I – love – you – I love – you!"

She was whispering the words that she had said a thousand times during the night but never thought that she could say them to him.

"I love you too," the Duke said. "Oh, my precious, my darling, what would have happened to me if I had never met you? *If* Shaw had never written *Pygmalion* and *if* your uncle and Archie Carnforth had not argued about it?"

"Perhaps it was – Fate that I – came – to Mere," Lorena said, "but I think Fate would have – brought us together anyway."

She gave him an entrancing little smile as she added,

"I might have saved you from being run over by a motor car or run down by an Express train!"

The Duke laughed.

"You have a lifetime to prevent any such things from happening to me, and I will protect you, my lovely one, from anything that might shock you. And that is a vow!"

"B-but – I cannot ask you to – change your whole life."

"You will not only change my life, but I know, because you are you and because, as you told me, the life force that you give out is a power for good and that you will change the lives of those who matter to us as friends. The others are of no account."

As he spoke, he thought of how Lorena had already altered the lives of the Marchioness of Trumpington and that of Jack Gilmour, how Kelvin Fane would now have something to occupy his mind other than 'flitting from *boudoir* to *boudoir*' and how Sir Hugo had unexpectedly found a new determination that might prevent his wife from behaving so badly in the future.

It was extraordinary what one small person could do just because she had the right ideas and perhaps, as she herself believed, she was helped by a Power given to her by God.

"Are you – sure – quite sure," Lorena asked, "that it would be – right for you to – marry me?"

"It would be everything that was wrong *not* to marry you!" the Duke replied. "But rightly or wrongly I have every intention of making you my wife and nothing and no one shall stop me!"

He spoke with a determination that made Lorena look at him admiringly.

"I love you – when you are like – that."

"Like what?" he asked.

"Strong and authoritative. I thought at first that it was rather – overwhelming – but it is how you should be. A leader – someone whom everyone looks up to and admires."

"You will make me conceited," the Duke smiled. "But I know, my darling, that I can be none of those things unless you are with me to show me how."

"That is – what I want," Lorena whispered, "but – "

"No buts," the Duke interrupted. "You want me to be authoritative and that is what I am! I intend to make you my wife as quickly as possible so that we can be together for always. Then we will teach each other about our love. As far as I am concerned, I think there is a great deal for me to learn."

He did not allow Lorena to answer.

His lips were now on hers and he was kissing her demandingly, insistently and a little more fiercely than he had done before as if he wished to make sure of her and allay some lingering fear within him that she might at the last moment escape him.

It seemed to Lorena as if the sun, as it had come burningly and crimson over the horizon that morning, was now on his lips and in his eyes.

Also, because he demanded it of her, she wanted to be closer and still closer to him, until she became an integral part of his body, his mind and his soul, as he was part of hers.

She knew that this was love as it should be, as her father had described it so often and what she had always prayed she might find one day.

It would not have mattered, she knew, if the man she loved had been a Duke or a pauper and, although she found Mere wonderful, it was the Duke who had filled her whole existence until in the midst of all his treasures she could see only him.

The Duke kissed her until she felt as if she had left the world behind and he had lifted her from the roof of Mere up into the sky and they were together in the heart of the sun.

"I love you! *God*, how I love you!" he exclaimed at length, his voice hoarse and unsteady.

"When will you marry me, my darling? I cannot wait to be sure of you and to have you with me both by day and by night."

"I am – ready to marry you now – at once," Lorena stammered.

He laughed.

"That is exactly what I wanted you to say, but I need to have a little time to arrange the Wedding and also, I presume, to ask for your uncle's permission."

He saw the expression on Lorena's face and asked her,

"What is worrying you?"

"You may think it – foolish of me, but I am afraid that if we have a – big Wedding with all your friends there, it will spoil what I – feel for you and what you – feel for me."

A little while ago, the Duke thought, he would not have understood what she was saying, but now he knew that the love he felt for Lorena was so precious, so sacred and its beauty was as fragile as the petal of a flower that nothing that was material or mundane must encroach upon it.

"When I – marry you," Lorena was saying in a very soft voice, "I want the Church to be filled with God and His love – not with – people."

"That is what you shall have, my precious," the Duke said. "We will be married the day after tomorrow in the Church where we prayed together on Sunday. Will that please you?"

"It would be wonderful!" Lorena exclaimed. "But – suppose Uncle Hugo does not – agree?"

"He *will* agree!" the Duke stated positively. "And there will be no need for you to go back to London on Thursday. I will arrange for a Special Licence and we need tell no one what we are doing until it is all over and you are *mine*."

Lorena realised that, although it was cowardly of her, she could not bear that Daisy Hellingford should have the chance of making a scene if she learnt that they were to be married.

She did not want the Duke's men-friends in their joking manner, laughing and talking about them.

But most of all, she did not want women like the Viscountess Storr and perhaps her aunt treating marriage as if it was something light and unimportant and not a Sacrament of Love, which her father had said it should always be.

The Duke was watching the expression in her eyes and then he assured her,

"Leave everything to me, my lovely one. I know what you are thinking and I feel the same. We will be married with only your uncle to give you away. Then I will take you for our honeymoon to a house I own by the sea, where we will be completely alone and can think only of ourselves."

Lorena gave a little cry of sheer delight.

Then she said,

"How can you be so wonderful? How can you understand all the things I want – and still be – you?"

"I understand you as you understand me," the Duke said. "That is because we belong to each other and have done so for many centuries of time."

"That is what I feel," Lorena replied with an ecstatic little sigh. "And I am so happy – so wildly crazily happy!"

She looked up at him and then murmured,

"Mr. Gillingham described this as a 'Fairy Palace' when I first saw it. Are you quite certain – it is real and I will not suddenly wake to find that this has all been a dream and you are, as you always have been – just the Prince Charming in my imagination?"

"I think, if I am in your dreams, you would be with me."

"I would want to be, but I do want to believe that you will really be my husband and me your wife."

"You can be sure of that," the Duke replied. "I knew, my darling, when you slipped your hand into mine as we stood on the roof, that I would never lose you and never let you go."

His lips were seeking hers again, kissing her fiercely and passionately. It did not make her afraid, it only aroused her in a way that she did not understand.

She felt as if his lips were awakening a strange fire that was seeping in flickering flames through her body, sweeping away her fears until they receded into an oblivion from which they would never return.

She put her arms round the Duke's neck and drew him closer still.

Everywhere there was Light – the Light of Love.

The Duke's lips became more insistent as her arms tightened round him.

"I love you! I love you – and you – are carrying me up into the sky," she whispered, "until in the whole world and in – the Universe there is nothing but – you!"

He looked down at her and he thought that the happiness in her face made him feel as if he too was lifted into the sky by the Divine Power of Love.

"I worship you, my precious," he said. "God has given you to me and now you will be mine through all Eternity."

It was a vow that came from his very soul and, as Lorena surrendered her lips to his again, she knew that this was the reality that they would never awaken from.

OTHER BOOKS IN THIS SERIES

The Barbara Cartland Eternal Collection is the unique opportunity to collect all five hundred of the timeless beautiful romantic novels written by the world's most celebrated and enduring romantic author.

Named the Eternal Collection because Barbara's inspiring stories of pure love, just the same as love itself, the books will be published on the internet at the rate of four titles per month until all five hundred are available.

The Eternal Collection, classic pure romance available worldwide for all time.